About the Author

Asha lives in a rural, quaint village. She was born in India but grew up in the Netherlands. From an early age, she loved losing herself in awe-inspiring books and stories. In her professional life, she has worked as a teacher in secondary education for quite some time now, hoping each day to inspire her students to read and enjoy books as much as she does. Most importantly, she encourages them to be kind and thoughtful, so everyone can be openly proud of who they are or who they're becoming. Asha is passionate about writing fiction with the LGBTQ+ community at its core. She is a published author of *All Queer but One*. Two more novels are set to be released later this year.

Me, Myself and Him

A. I. Rebel-Lammersen

Me, Myself and Him

Olympia Publishers
London

www.olympiapublishers.com
OLYMPIA PAPERBACK EDITION

Copyright © A. I. Rebel-Lammersen 2024

The right of A. I. Rebel-Lammersen to be identified as author of this work has been asserted in accordance with sections 77 and 78 of the Copyright, Designs and Patents Act 1988.

All Rights Reserved

No reproduction, copy or transmission of this publication
may be made without written permission.
No paragraph of this publication may be reproduced,
copied or transmitted save with the written permission of the publisher,
or in accordance with the provisions
of the Copyright Act 1956 (as amended).

Any person who commits any unauthorised act in relation to this publication may be liable to criminal prosecution and civil claims for damage.

A CIP catalogue record for this title is
available from the British Library.

ISBN: 978-1-83543-115-3

This is a work of fiction.
Names, characters, places and incidents originate from the writer's imagination. Any resemblance to actual persons, living or dead, is purely coincidental.

First Published in 2024

Olympia Publishers
Tallis House
2 Tallis Street
London
EC4Y 0AB

Printed in Great Britain

Dedication

I dedicate this book to my loving, diverse and colourful family: Willem, Julian and Benjamin. You guys are the wind beneath my wings.

Acknowledgements

I'd like to thank Willem for his encouragement while writing this book and for helping me pursue my dreams. Thanks for all the pre-reading late at night, even after a hard day's work. Hugs and kisses to my two handsome sons, Julian and Benjamin. You've been so patient with Mummy while she locked herself up for hours on end to write. Thanks to my parents, Jan and Ans, for their unwavering support. Thank you to the rest of my family (Deepa, Mark, Noa, Lev, Grada, Jan Sr., Jack, Joa, Jan Jr., Steffanie and gorgeous little Syb) for cheering me on from the sidelines. A special thanks to my sister-in-law, Marianne, for being so incredibly supportive and excited for me from the onset of this amazing journey, and for understanding from personal experience how challenging it is to pursue a career in the arts. My dear Hilde, I cannot stress enough how much your friendship, love and support mean to me. Your light shines so unbelievably bright. Thanks for everything. I'd like to thank Olympia Publishers for taking a chance on me, and for helping me proofread and edit my manuscript. Last but not least, I'd like to thank the LGBTQIA2S+ community for inspiring me. I hope you all get to live beautiful and fulfilling lives. Remember; you matter, you're important, and you're awesome.

Kobe Dewinter

Being me is pretty great, if I say so myself. I've got loads of mates, I'm easy on the eyes, and I'm top scorer of my soccer team. School isn't exactly my forte, but most of my teachers don't give me a hard time about that. Except for my art teacher, Mr Blend, also known as Mr Bell End. A clever little nickname I came up with, and I made sure it would catch on with the rest of the student population. It only took a couple of eager-to-please ninth graders to pen that name down all over the walls of our scruffy toilet cubicles. And once a name picks up, it sticks to you like glue, at least for as long as I am around. And well, that is debatable at the moment, I'm afraid.

Not that it's any of my fault, really; that little grass, Paquito or Pussyto, as I'd like to call him, ratted me out to Mr Bell End. And what for? It was just a little prank among schoolmates. Colour-sprayed a couple of knobs on those ridiculous rainbow flags Pussyto's been flaunting about with. He's been decorating like mad for our school's Coming Out Day. Way over the top, if you ask me. It's bad enough being a sissy, but celebrating and sharing it with the whole school? That is next-level nasty. Ever since that Gender-Sexuality-Alliance was founded, it's been purple Fridays and queer flags all over the place. Just the other day, he asked me to join them in front of my entire soccer team. Naturally, I said no to their GSA, or Gay-Stupid-Annoying, as I call them. To put a little emphasis on that promise, I spray-painted boners on those rainbow flags for good measure. They should be thanking me, really; you can practically pass my artwork off as a Banksy, especially since I drew a very resembling pic of Paquito on one of those flags, nerdy specs and all. Mr Blend, who oversees the GSA, reported me to the principal, so that's where I am now. In his office, waiting for my parents to arrive. I've had better days, to be honest.

Jai Patel-Jones

My first name means victory, although I'm not feeling very victorious right now. In fact, I feel rather lame, having been stood up for the second time this week. Looking at my reflection in a Mason & Mason shop window, I notice that my lips have turned blue. It's not a good sign, but it's perfectly understandable after waiting for thirty minutes on a chilly afternoon. I was supposed to have tea and scones with my boyfriend Josh, but he just bailed out. Looking at the text he sent me, I try to change his words with willpower. Of course, that doesn't work out for me either, so I just keep staring at them over and over again.

So sorry to keep you waiting; I am stuck at rehearsals.
I'll make it up to you.
See you at school! Hugs, Josh.

He always signs off with his name, which is pretty redundant if you ask me. Your name and profile picture are visible, after all. Josh's profile pic is one I keep falling head over heels for every time I see it. His dazzling smile, cute dimples and messy blond hair give him that just-out-of-bed look I like so much. Just by looking at that photo, I've already forgiven him for cancelling our date for the second time this week. I am lucky to have his affection in the first place. Josh is quite the man at Stonewall High. Captain of the debate club, co-director of our school's play, and not doing badly on the handball team either.

The play's performance is less than a month away, and

although he tries to hide it, he's pretty stressed out. As a supportive boyfriend, I should be lenient with his quirks, like not showing up for a date again. And even though I know he won't check in with me before Monday, I'll respect his busy schedule and give him the space he needs. Maybe he'll make it up to me by finally taking a profile pic together, one we can both use on WhatsApp. I've been dreaming about that for some time now. Just the two of us, side by side or cheek by cheek, smiling at the camera and letting every contact on our phones know we're a happy couple. Yes, that's what I'll suggest next time I see him. After all, he owes me.

Kobe Dewinter

"Thank you for coming, Mrs Dewinter. I really appreciate you taking the time to join us."

We're in the principal's office. My mum fidgets with her purse, zipping it open and closed and looking at its contents every few seconds. In the end, she settles down.

"My husband could not make it, I'm afraid; he is tied up at a meeting."

Mr Calhoon looks over his spectacles and sighs quietly.

"I understand, Mrs Dewinter; his schedule must be packed."

My father is a well-known figure in our city; he's the deputy mayor. We don't get to see a lot of him, and when he is home, he retires to his office to watch soccer. When we do speak, the conversation is mostly limited to his favourite topics; my grades, dates and Mr Bates. The latter is my soccer coach, because God forbid, Mr Bates doesn't see my potential or forgets using it to bag another win in our team's soccer league. I think my performance on the soccer pitch won't be on today's agenda, though.

"Perhaps Kobe has brought you up to date on why I asked you to come to school today, Mrs Dewinter."

Mum clears her throat and speaks quietly.

"Well, Mr Calhoon, he hasn't. I was at work when you phoned me, and since my job takes a lot of focus, I do not usually speak to Kobe when at work."

Mum works as the head of the financial department of a law

firm downtown. Even though they don't work her to the bone and she doesn't pull all-nighters, she spends most of her time over there. Who can blame her – a husband who's never home and a teenage son whom she is called to school for in the middle of the day?

"Very well," Mr Calhoon chimes in. "Kobe has vandalised school property, which is, as far as I am concerned, absolutely unacceptable."

"And what might this vandalised property exactly entail, Mr Calhoon?"

Mum shifts slightly in her seat but doesn't break eye contact.

"Rainbow flags, to be used as decoration for our school's Coming Out Day this Friday."

"I see; I'm happy to reimburse you for these flags, Mr Calhoon. Please let my assistant know what we owe you."

Now, Mr Calhoon starts shifting in his chair.

"Mrs De Winter, I appreciate the offer, but we have to address Kobe's behaviour as well, which is, at best, disappointing."

Mum starts fidgeting with her purse again before she focuses on Mr Calhoon.

"As far as I know, Mr Calhoon, your job is to run this school to the best of your ability. Is your best ability getting worked up about a teenage boy pushing back a little at your Rainbow Day Out?"

"It's our school's Coming Out Day, Mrs Dewinter," squeaks Mr Calhoon.

"Semantics, Mr Calhoon. When you wanted to renovate and refurbish this school, my husband endorsed your plans and helped out in getting you all the permits you needed. I expect you to be helpful in return."

Mr Calhoon slowly turns red but keeps his composure.

"Mrs Dewinter, we are grateful for all that your husband has done for this school. Nonetheless, this incident will have consequences for Kobe. Next Saturday, after our Coming Out Day, he will help our janitor clean up."

Now it's my turn to butt in.

"I can't be here on Saturday, Mr Calhoon; I have a soccer game. If we win this game, we're basically guaranteed the championship title."

"Well, time is not on your side, Kobe. It's something to think about if you ever feel the need to vandalise school property again. Oh, and a no-show means expulsion; this isn't your first offence, unfortunately."

I look at Mum to back me up, but she looks bored and annoyed.

"Mr Calhoon, I've spent too much time on trivial matters as it is; I really need to be going. Kobe will be here on Saturday."

And without so much as a goodbye, she saunters out of the office.

Jai Patel-Jones

I wake up to the smell of freshly baked muffins. My pops bakes them every Saturday, and I'm grateful for it. Especially after Josh stood me up again on Friday night. I spent my whole Saturday revising for upcoming exams and fantasising about our perfect couple's profile pic. Only one more day before I get to see him again and share my thoughts on where and when we should take it. But first, a mug of hot, steaming coffee and, by the smell of it, blueberry muffins. When I come down for breakfast, my dads are sitting at the table. Vikram is skimming the newspaper, and Robin is in the kitchen stacking plates in the dishwasher.

"Morning, love, you're an early riser," Dad says, peering over his paper. "What has gotten you up and about this early?"

"It's nearly nine. I don't want to be late for today's Kiki. I'm feeling inspired."

"Woah," Pops says. "Only yesterday you were moping around the house over Josh; quite rude he stood you up again, isn't it?"

"We're fine; he's just really busy with that school play. Less than a month to go, and it's his debut as a director."

"Okay, if you say so, darling. It's just that I would hate to see you get hurt. You are so invested in Josh, and I sometimes wonder if he feels the same about you."

"Don't worry, Pops. Josh and I are going to get our profile pic taken together, can't get more invested than that."

"Wow, sharing a profile pic – that's quite something. Our

boy is growing up, Robin. Do you remember when we started taking profile pics together? I was so nervous for our first one, I ended up smiling like a deranged hyena."

"Oh, Vikram, you looked fine in that picture; I, on the other hand, had a bad hair day. It was sticking up on all sides, even after tonnes of hairspray and wax."

"In other words, son, don't get too worked up about your first profile pic with Josh; many more will follow, and each one will look better than the last."

"Thanks, Dad," I say, licking the last blueberry muffin crumbs off my fingers.

"Will Josh be at the Kiki today?"

"No, Pops, he has back-to-back rehearsals all weekend. But I'll probably see Selma and Jess there."

Selma, Jess and I have been besties since elementary school. I had a hard time fitting in since I wore an eye patch due to a lazy eye. The slight lisp in my speech didn't do me any favours, either. Selma and Jess were the only ones who did not treat me like a dysfunctional pirate with a speech impediment. In fact, they often let me be the hero in our made-up stories about knights, dragons and princesses that needed rescuing.

Although Selma always insisted on being the knight to rescue her damsel in distress, Jess. Eyepatch or not, even I could see that these two were soulmates. They've been dating for a couple of months now. Something that felt inevitable to all of us but still took some time getting used to. At first, Selma and Jess were terrified that if it didn't work out, it would be the end of their friendship. I was worried I'd become a third wheel, but it turned out nothing much changed. We still see each other all the time, and when we don't, we text or FaceTime. I've had quite a few missed calls from Jess and a dozen texts from Selma, which all come down to the same question: How was your date with Josh?

I'll see them at the Kiki in less than an hour, the perfect place to spill the beans on my so-called love life. Although I'm not looking forward to filling them in on another failed date with my beau, I can't wait to see them. Our Sunday morning gatherings, also known as Kiki, take place in our town hall. Most families attend faithfully each week. Afterwards, there is a brunch with food and snacks that we all bring. Since most families are into baking and showing off their treats, it's a feast for the eyes. Pops usually brings his signature blueberry muffins, which work wonders as comfort food and are a great conversation starter.

Kobe Dewinter

After I've left Mr Calhoon's office, I feel a rage building inside me. Missing the most important match of the season because of some whiny little wimp grassing. Pussyto's spray-painted flags are the least of his problems when I'm done with him. Luckily, I can always count on my bros to have my back. Jake and Roy have been texting me like mad ever since I set foot in the principal's office. I'm not even halfway down the hall when they flank me, immediately firing away their questions.

"Bro, what's up? Why were you in Calhoon's office? Was that your mum I saw?" Roy says in one breath.

"Are you in trouble? It's not about those stupid queer flags, right?" Jake nearly shouts.

After I've given them an update, they settle down a little.

"Kobe, this is so unfair; you can't miss Saturday's match; we can't win without you."

"Relax, Roy; I'm not planning on bailing out. My dad will talk to Cahoon and sort this out. He's way too invested in my soccer career to let this slide."

"Uhm, Kobe, has Mr Calhoon said anything about us?"

"Why would he have, Jake? Do you think I've told him that you guys helped me create the artwork on those flags? I would never tell on you if that's what you're afraid of."

"Of course not, Kobe; you're not a grass like Pussyto. Speaking of which, do you want to wait for him after school? There's a little spray paint left, and I'm sure that specky sod could use a makeover."

"No, Roy, I'll deal with him later; he won't get away with this."

When I get home, I see my dad's car parked in our driveway. I'm surprised to find him in the kitchen well before dinnertime.

"Dad, good to see you. How was your day?"

"Not much better than yours, I'm afraid. Elections are coming up soon, and we've lost quite a lot of endorsements. We need all hands on deck now, or I'm out of a job sooner rather than later."

"Sorry to hear that, but if you can spare a moment, there's been a misunderstanding at school. I need you to talk to Mr Calhoon for me."

"Yes, your mother filled me in on that, Kobe. Terrible shame you are going to miss Saturday's game with your potential."

"Wait, what? Aren't you going to put in a good word for me with Calhoon? I can't miss that game; it's a decisive match."

"Kobe, as much as I would love to, Mr Calhoon is a prominent and influential person in this town; I need his endorsement.

"And it won't look particularly good if the deputy mayor's son gets expelled at this point in the campaign. Listen, I agree with you on all that queer-promoting silliness that goes on at your school. For heaven's sake, what more do they want? But truth be told, I can't afford to be on his bad side now. I expect you to be at school on Saturday."

My dad grabs a turkey sandwich and heads in a straight line for his study. Guess that's that, then. I will miss the match and spend my Saturday cleaning up after queers. Great, life just couldn't get any better.

Jai Patel-Jones

We leave our house perfectly colour-coordinated. All three of us enjoy dressing up a bit for town gatherings, and what better way to do so than by choosing similar colours and patterns in our outfits? We're all going for navy blue this week. Dad is wearing a navy-blue sports coat, Pops is sporting navy blue chinos underneath a white shirt, and I'm in a navy-blue V-neck with a tiny anchor printed on the top left of my shirt.

When we pass the Smiths', their beagles start barking at us.

"Must be those delicious muffins you baked, Robin," Dad says.

"Bye, Laura; bye, Ann, are we going to see you at today's Kiki?" Pops yells over their fence.

The Smiths are still in their nightgowns, trying to shush their dogs.

"We'll be there in a minute, overslept a bit I'm afraid," Laura yells back over the noise their feisty beagle Maeve produces.

"Would be a first if they were on time this week," Dad mutters under his breath.

On our way to the city town hall, we run into most of our friends and acquaintances. Mr and Mr Hubert from Greenwich Lane, Mrs and Mrs Bassey from Christopher Street, and Chris and Frank with their gorgeous baby girl Lizzie.

"Is she sleeping through the night, Chris?" Dad inquires.

"I'm afraid she isn't," Chris answers. "She is a little night crawler. Keeps me up and about till three a.m., but since I am still on paternity leave, I catch up with sleep during the day."

Right now, little Lizzie is peacefully snoring on Chris's shoulder while Frank is pushing her stroller. When we get to our town hall, also known as the Malcolm Michaels Centre, most people have already poured in. We take our usual seats at the back, near the aisle, so Pops can watch and greet everyone coming in after us. After everyone settles down, Mr Phillips starts this week's Kiki by welcoming everyone and thanking them for coming. Every Kiki begins with a series of town-related announcements, usually about renovations on public buildings, landscaping plans, or noteworthy intel on someone's life.

"This week's bouquet goes to Mrs and Mrs Kaiser, who will celebrate their fortieth wedding anniversary next week."

Everyone applauds and tries to catch a glimpse of the happy couple holding hands in one of the front rows. When the announcements are done, Mr Phillips, who's one of the key note speakers at the centre, delivers an inspiring speech on what it really means to love thy neighbour. He ends his speech by using one of his favourite quotes by this centre's namesake, Malcolm Michaels, also known as Marsha P. Johnson.

Each Kiki ends with all of us singing a song from our hymnbook called Love Is Love. Mrs Kent accompanies us on the piano. We all stand and sing one of my favourites from Katrina and the Waves: *Love Shine a Light*. When Mrs Kent hits her final notes, people start gathering their stuff, eager to leave and start brunch. Baked goods, sandwiches and other delicious foods are left on big tables at the back of the entrance hall.

From the corner of my eye, I see Selma and Jess waving at me to come over and join them. I can't wait to start digging into some of that dim sum the Li-Zhang family brought with them, preferably with a side dish of town gossip.

Kobe Dewinter

I am clutching a mop, trying to clean the school's confetti-strewn hallways. Dad dropped me off at eight thirty sharp. Wouldn't even let me lie in for an hour or so. Since he has meetings all day, he wanted to leave early. He thinks that if I hurry up, I might still be on time to catch the second half of the game. Fat chance, though, with this mess.

Even when I have finished down here, there are about two dozen rainbow flags to take down, lipstick-covered mirrors to scrub, and purple nail polish to scrape off about fifteen desks.

Our janitor, Mr Fairview, is taking his sweet time drinking his third cup of coffee. Just because I was assigned to help him, he treats me as a juvenile delinquent. He stares at me with his beady eyes and shouts across the hallway.

"Get a move on, Dewinter; those flags aren't going to come down on their own."

"Perhaps you could give me a hand, Mr Fairview," I bite back.

"Well, have I ever? You're not here for the afterparty, Dewinter. And do I need to remind you that leaving early equals not coming back at all?"

I take a deep breath and bite my lower lip to stop me from really laying into that imp. I would love to give him a piece of my mind, but of course, he is right. If I screw this up, it's a one-way ticket out of this school. And probably my house too, 'cause Dad is never going to forgive me for all the bad press my expulsion will get his campaign. Besides, I can't afford to miss any more school. Had a little too much fun last year and failed most of my exams. It has cost me more than an extra year of high school; my girlfriend, Dana, broke up with me. We were together for two years and were madly inseparable. Dana graduated last year and moved on to university. We tried to make it work at first, but she claimed I was holding her back from new, exciting experiences. So, she's probably off having wild adventures with some college frat boy while I'm stuck here with a sweaty, balding, middle-aged janitor. I'll just have to suck it up for now, pass my exams, and get the hell out of this suffocating town. I have no plans of going to college. My mum promised to buy me an airline ticket to any place I wanted to go if I graduated. I'm planning on taking a gap year to go backpacking through Australia. I'll take on any odd job they'll throw at me to pay for a crash pad and some chow. Hopefully, that will keep me going for at least a year. After that, I'll just see where life takes me.

My daydreaming is rudely interrupted by my phone buzzing. It's halftime, and Jake is keeping me up-to-date. My team is behind 0-2 and really needs to step up to secure the championship title. I scroll through his messages, in which he mostly begs me to ditch the old fart, Mr Fairview, and make it to the second half. I am sorely tempted, but I just can't. There is more at stake than a soccer championship. After I'm done with the confetti, I move on to scrubbing mirrors. Thankfully, Mr Fairview has finally decided to make himself useful and is taking down rainbow flags. I grab a scouring pad from my overflowing bucket of soapy water and start working on the nearest mirror. It has a big, pink lipstick-drawn heart on it, claiming 'Love is for everyone'. Except for me, I think. To add insult to injury, the lipstick won't come off, no matter how hard I scrub. The top left corner is just out of reach. I push myself up on the sink to get that last bit of pink removed. Don't want to give Fairview any reason to complain and keep me here longer than necessary. Maintenance is clearly not a priority at this school, which becomes clear to me when the sink comes away from the wall it's supposed to be attached to. I land on my butt, precariously balancing the sink on my lap. I look up at the mirror. That annoying speck of pink is still there, and it's becoming bigger. Too late, I realise the mirror has come unhinged and is plummeting my way. When I look up at my reflection, I see someone else. Long black eyelashes covering hazel brown eyes are staring back at me.

The slight pout of his lips stands out in his chestnut-coloured face. Deep brown curls frame his delicate features. Right before the mirror hits me square in the face, it dawns on me that I must have gone insane.

Jai Patel-Jones

When the alarm clock wakes me up on Monday morning, I practically tumble out of bed in a hurry to get dressed. Today, I get to see Josh again. We haven't really been in touch over the weekend, but Selma assured me he was kept at rehearsals 24/7. Being a co-director means you don't get any time off. Selma has first-hand intel about that because her brother Jaimy is co-directing the play with him. According to Selma, Jaimy has shown his face once this weekend to take a quick shower and change into some clean clothes. I'm proud of my hard-working boyfriend, maybe I will surprise him with a picnic at the park this weekend. While getting dressed, I picture myself putting together an amazing spread for us to enjoy. Scones, hand-made petit fours, and I'll ask Pops to bake his blueberry muffins. Maybe I can even sneak out a bottle of Prosecco. Dad lets me sip wine on weekends, and Pops occasionally shares a beer with me. We won't get sloshed, though, just a little drink to celebrate his awesomeness as a director and, of course, to celebrate us. The park will be a great place to take our first shared profile pic. I even know the perfect spot. There's this quaint wooden bridge over a small stream of water. It's an eye-catching landmark and has been around for a very long time. The bridge is in dilapidated condition and will be up for renovation soon. It definitely has to be this weekend, then. Downstairs, I gulp down a glass of milk and grab a piece of bacon from Dad's plate. Despite his pleas to sit down and have a proper breakfast, I'm already halfway out the door. If I hurry up, I can still catch Josh before our first class. After I've parked and locked my bike, I head straight for the auditorium. That's where Josh hangs out most of the time when he isn't in class. Even when the auditorium is not being used for rehearsals, the vibe inspires him. It gives him a chance to review decisions he's made or visualise new ideas for the next rehearsal. I don't want to startle Josh when he might be in the middle of some serious thought process, so I don't knock and enter quietly.

"This is not working out; this is not going to end well," Josh is muttering.

Then someone else chips in.

"Come on, let's give it another shot; we can't just leave things like this."

"Enough is enough; this will affect the show. I'm pulling the plug." Wow, one of the cast members is in serious trouble; why else would Josh tell someone off like that? I'm about to make my presence known when Jaimy comes into view. He wraps his arms around Josh and holds him tight.

"Aren't you going to miss all the benefits?"

He leans in and kisses Josh. Pulling the plug is clearly not on Josh's mind. When I hear a soft moan escape his mouth, I gasp. They finally noticed me. There is neither rhyme nor reason to this. This cannot be happening. But it is. And I just have to get out of here. As I turn around and flee the auditorium, the bell rings to announce the start of the first period. I jump on my bike and start pedalling. I don't even know where I'm going; my vision is blurred by tears streaming down my face.

Somehow, I end up at the entrance of the park. I get off my bike and start walking. This is where we are supposed to have our romantic picnic this weekend. This gorgeous bridge would have been ideal for our first profile pic. But none of that is going to happen. I lean over the bridge and peer into the water below, hoping to find answers to all the questions I have. Instead, I'm looking at my own sad reflection until I realise it isn't me. Bright blue eyes are looking up at me underneath blond, cropped hair, combed back with a proper scoop of wax. His full, rosy lips are slightly parted. I turn around to see who's behind me, but no one is. I look back at the water and lean in a bit more. That's when the railing gives way. This is the worst day ever.

Kobe Dewinter

My head's throbbing, and my throat feels like sandpaper. I carefully open my eyes and expect to see Mr Fairview hovering over me. Instead, I hear quiet whispers. Two men are slowly coming into focus. They have their backs turned to me, but I can still make out what they're saying.

"He's lucky Laura and Ann found him while walking their dogs in the park," one of them says.

"I still don't understand what he was doing there at this time of day; he's supposed to be at school," the other one adds.

"Could it have anything to do with Josh? He has about a dozen missed calls from him."

"I don't know, Vikram; let's ask him when he wakes up. The doctor says he made a bad fall from that horrid bridge. He really needs to take it easy for a while."

"Let's go downstairs, Robin; I'll check in on him after lunch."

They leave, and I'm fully awake now. I look around and notice that I'm in someone else's bedroom, or, to be precise, in someone else's bed. The walls are covered in posters. Leo and Kate are doing their classic *Titanic* pose, Timothée Chalamet is smiling at the cameras on the red carpet, and then there is a music poster from a band called Katrina and the Waves. This is definitely not my room.

And who are those two men talking about me? They can't be paramedics since I am not at the hospital. And they sounded way too involved and worried. I sit up straight and feel as if a thousand needles are stabbing me in the face. Ouch, I really need to take it easy. I manage to get out of bed and head towards a vanity table at the back of the room. It has a large mirror framed by soft, glowing lights. I look at my reflection and realise for the second time that it's not me. An Indian boy is staring back at me, with the same hazelnut brown eyes and deep brown curls I saw before that mirror hit me in the face. I take a closer look. I'm in blue striped satin pyjamas with little cufflinks on the sleeves. I'm slender-built, with no discernible muscle tone. My feet are small and fit perfectly well into a pair of fluffy red slippers next to the bed. I cannot wrap my head around this, but I seem to be someone else. At least my body is; I do remember who I am. Kobe Dewinter, a star soccer player, has loads of friends, and is not in the mood for any shenanigans. Because this simply can't be real.

"Jai, you're awake; how are you feeling?"

I turn around and see one of the men I heard earlier. He looks a bit like me – an older version, that is. I don't know what to say without freaking out completely, so I keep quiet.

"Robin, he's up! Come have a look."

"Oh, Vikram, he looks terribly under the weather. Should we call Dr Said again?"

"Let's wait and see how he feels in a couple of hours. He's only been up for a minute or so."

They both stare at me, and I realise I have to say something.

"Uhm, I'm fine; it's just that my head hurts a bit."

"Of course, it does. You're lucky you're not in the hospital, isn't he, Vikram?"

"There, there, Robin, no need to scare the boy. The water broke most of his fall, but you did take quite a tumble off that bridge."

"Why don't you get back in bed, Jai? I'll make you some blueberry muffins," Robin offers.

Vikram lingers at the door and clears his throat.

"Jai, if you're ready to talk about what happened between you and Josh, I'm here for you."

He takes one final look at me, and then he's gone too.

Jai Patel-Jones

A chilly sensation rushes through my face as I slowly come around. I'm spread-eagled on the floor. The cold bathroom tiles are causing me to shiver relentlessly. I'm surrounded by soapy puddles of water, and a damaged sink rests between my legs. I haven't had much time to consider my predicament. An elderly man looms over me, peering angrily at me.

"Well, Dewinter, congratulations. You made an even bigger mess than those queer kids left me with on Friday. And damaged school property again. We might as well take up extra insurance as long as you're around, boy. Which I doubt is for long. I called your mum; she'll be here any minute. Clean yourself up a bit; you look like a train wreck."

To be honest, that's exactly how I feel. I feel bruised all over and can barely get on my feet. The elderly man has left and is nowhere to be seen. I must have heard him wrong, but it did sound like he said my mum would be here shortly. I have two dads, not two mums, so he probably said that because he was annoyed with me. I can imagine why: the bathroom I'm in looks utterly destroyed. But he can't honestly think I did that. The last thing I remember is falling off a bridge after I bolted from the auditorium. Then it hits me like a wave: Josh, the love of my life, is with someone else. This is all too much to handle. I sit down again and wrap my arms around my legs. Then I hear high heels clicking my way. A lady wearing an elegant side-slit skirt suit is towering over me. She squats next to me and grabs my arm.

"Kobe, what on earth is going on? I got a call from Mr Fairview telling me you smashed up a bathroom."

I have no idea who Kobe is or why she calls me that, but I answer anyway.

"I didn't do this; I fell and hurt my head; that's all I remember."

The woman takes in the wrecked bathroom. The elderly man, whom she called Mr Fairview, suddenly appears in the doorway.

"Mrs Dewinter, as you can see, there's substantial damage to this bathroom."

"Yes, I can see that, Mr Fairview. I just wonder how it's possible that both a sink and a mirror can nearly bludgeon my son to death. It sounds like some serious deferred maintenance to me. You'll be hearing from our attorney, Mr Fairview. If you will excuse me, I'd like to get my son home."

Mr Fairview turns a bright shade of red but keeps quiet. I have a massive headache, but I understand this lady is going to take me home. I can't wait to see Dad and crawl into bed with some of Pop's famous comfort food. I follow her to the parking lot, trying to keep up. She walks surprisingly fast on those kitten heels of hers. The drive doesn't take long. We pull up on a long, rutted driveway. The bumpy ride doesn't help my throbbing headache, so I'm glad when we walk up to the house.

"So, is my dad going to pick me up here?" I ask the lady.

"What are you talking about, dear? Your father has meetings all day. We're lucky if we get to see him at all today."

I have no idea what she means by that. Both my dads would drop anything in a split second if they knew I needed them. We enter the house, and the lady walks me up a flight of stairs.

"It's best if you lie down for a while, darling. You look rather pale, and I'm not sure you don't have a concussion."

She opens a bedroom door. I'm about to object because I really need to get going now. My dads will be so worried. The lady has left, and I'm here on my own. Right, I'll just call Dad then; he always takes my calls. I walk into the bedroom for some privacy. There's a drum kit in the corner. On the walls are posters showing famous soccer players in action, except for the one hanging over the bed. It's a photo of a scantily dressed Kendall Jenner posing provocatively. Clearly, I'm in her daughter's bedroom, but why does she think I'm her son? There's a standing mirror next to the wardrobe. Since my face feels badly bruised, I take a quick look.

That bright-eyed boy I saw on the bridge this morning is staring back at me. I touch my face, and so does he. I take a good look at myself. Baggy jeans, a white T, and a checkered shirt. A pair of flashy Jordans are on my feet. Who in the world is this guy?

Kobe Dewinter

I spend most of my day in bed. Vikram and Robin keep bringing me hot chocolate, chamomile tea, and lots of baked treats. So far, I have figured out that I'm not me. Well, I am still Kobe, but I'm in another dude's skin. And not just his skin; his life too. I have already ruled out that I'm dreaming 'cause it's been hours since I first woke up. Since when do dreams hurt? My head is still aching. Around eleven, I hear Vikram and Robin stumbling upstairs, talking quietly so as not to wake me up.

"He seemed really out of sorts today, Robin. Like he didn't know who he was or where he was. I think we should take him to the hospital first thing in the morning. I don't like this at all."

"You're probably right, darling. He took quite a fall, and we can't take any risks. He hasn't mentioned Josh at all, which is odd, to say the least. I talked to Mrs Murphy at the pharmacy today, Selma's mum. She said that Jaimy was in quite a state because something happened between the three of them at school."

"I thought so too, love. Let's not bother Jai with that; he'll talk to us when he's ready."

Great, this dude Jai is mixed up in some sort of love triangle with two other dudes. Not surprised to learn he's gay, seeing how he's decorated his room. But what are the odds of two gay men raising a queer kid? Did I die and go to hell? Can't wait to get out of here. But first, I need to figure out how. That is not going to happen if I'm stuck at the hospital being examined and questioned by doctors. They'll probably find out sooner rather than later that I don't know anything about my life, or, to be more precise Jai's. It's highly unlikely Vikram and Robin will let me walk around town with amnesia. I'll have to come up with a plan tomorrow.

I'm exhausted and sleep well into the next morning. Vikram shows up carrying a breakfast tray topped with enough food to feed half of my soccer team. After I've polished off a good deal, Robin returns for the empty tray.

"Listen, I'm feeling much better today; the headache is practically gone. I was thinking of taking a little stroll downtown, just to get some fresh air."

"I don't know, love; you were very poorly yesterday. Dad and I are taking you to the hospital for another check-up. Just to make sure you're all right."

Oh no, I can't let that happen; I have to talk my way out of this.

"Listen, things got really messy between me and Josh yesterday, and I need some space."

I understand, love; you can go for a walk after we've been to the hospital."

I really have to give it my all now.

"No, I don't want to go to the hospital!" I shout at him. I'm blinking like mad to get some tears flowing.

"I'm fine; all I need is some time alone to organise my thoughts. I won't be gone long, just for an hour or so."

Robin stares at me open-mouthed; he's clearly not used to outbursts from Jai. Just as I think that I made things worse, he relents.

"Fine, you can go out for a walk, but just around the neighbourhood. Why don't you ask Selma or Jess to join you?

They're dying to know how you are doing."

"I need some time alone, but I'll text them. I'll be back in an hour."

"Half an hour, Jai, and before you go, take a shower."

When Robin has left, I get up. The man has a point; I do reek. Jai's room has an en suite with a bath and shower. Lined up neatly, I spot shower gel, body wash, body lotion, three different shampoos, and a big bottle of conditioner. Not to mention, he has three loofah sponges in a little basket. This dude takes personal hygiene to the next level. But it is nice to have a shower. I undress and take a look at myself. I miss seeing my six-pack and muscular arms.

I'm slim to the point of being skinny. And a lot hairier, except for my southern borders. It's a shaven haven down there, but with a substantial ship, the lucky bastard. After my shower, I get dressed. Jai's clothes are a bit campy, so I settle for a pair of navy-blue chinos and a black shirt. Vikram and Robin are at the kitchen table.

"Half an hour, Jai. Keep your phone with you."

I grab Jai's phone off the kitchen counter and leave before they change their mind.

Jai Patel-Jones

I've never had a panic attack before, so I don't know what one feels like. But if I had to guess, it's what I'm feeling right now. My hands are clammy, my mouth is dry, and I'm breathing heavily. My vision is blurry, and I think I'm about to pass out. A firm knock on the door brings me back to my senses. Two guys my age walk in. One is looking at me curiously; the other one looks slightly concerned.

"Kobe, we heard what happened. Are you all right, dude?"

It takes me a second to realise that I'm Kobe.

"Uhm, yes, it's been quite the day so far."

The other guy chimes in. "Dude, Roy and I dropped by at school as soon as the game was over. You weren't there, and Fairview was in a right state. He kept screeching at the top of his lungs that you vandalised school property again. If it were up to him, you wouldn't come back there."

"He was in a proper rage, right, Jake?"

"Furious as hell, Roy."

I don't know what to say to them, but luckily, Jake isn't finished.

"We reckoned you were sent home; ergo, our next stop. Your mum let us in; she said you slipped and fell. How's your head, by the way?"

That's a question I can answer truthfully.

"Quite bad, to be honest."

"We lost today's game, Kobe."

"I'm sorry to hear that," I say politely.

"Hope you'll be up and running in time for our last match."

"Don't bother him about the game, Jake; he looks awful and probably feels that way too."

"All I'm saying, Roy, is that if Kobe had been there, we wouldn't have lost. But what's done is done. Hey Kobe, how about we take things slow today, watch a movie, have a couple of beers, and order some pizzas?"

I feel that's about all I can take on today, so I nod.

"I'll go downstairs to score a couple of brew skis."

"And that'll be the only thing he'll score today," snorts Roy.

"I wouldn't be so pleased with myself, Roy; my gran could have put up a better defence on that pitch." Judging by the back-and-forth banter, Jake, Roy, and Kobe are close friends.

"Hey, Kobe, why don't you get the movie started, your pick today."

I turn to where Jake points and notice a vast collection of DVDs. The entire series of *Lethal Weapon, Naked Gun, Karate Kid and Saw* are neatly organised on a bottom shelf.

"Uhm, Roy, do you remember where I put my copy of *The Notebook*?"

"The what?" Roy replies.

"*The Notebook*, or maybe *Eat, Pray, Love*?"

"I don't think you have any of those, Kobe; you're really into action movies."

"Oh, right," I say.

It's beyond me why Kobe doesn't have any of the classics, but I settle for a *Karate Kid* movie. After the pizzas have arrived, I'm starting to feel a bit better. Didn't realise how famished I was until now. I haven't had anything to eat since breakfast, and that was just a piece of bacon I snatched off of Dad's plate.

Thinking about home hits me hard. I don't want to choke up in front of Roy and Jake, so I shove another slice of pepperoni in my mouth. After the movie, I'm spent. I try to suppress a huge yawn and fail miserably. Luckily, Jake and Roy take the hint and leave.

"Now you go and get some rest, Kobe," Roy says.

"Yep, we'll see ourselves out," adds Jake.

"We'll figure out on Monday how to get back at that little snitch, Pussyto."

I have no idea what they're on about, but I'm too exhausted to find out. I give them a little wave as they leave Kobe's bedroom. All I want is a hot shower and a good night's sleep. Who knows maybe I'll wake up from this nightmare in the morning.

Kobe's bathroom is small but clean. I can't find his shower cap, so I'll just have to blow-dry my hair then. There are two nearly identical bottles in a plastic shower caddy. One label reads body wash; the other one reads shampoo. There isn't a loofah in sight. Thank goodness the water is scalding hot, just the way I like it. As I soap up with Kobe's body wash, I notice my body is quite muscular. I've never had a six-pack, so I let my hands run freely, using my fingertips to explore all there is. I dig up a plastic razor from the caddy.

Whatever he uses it for is a mystery to me since it's practically the Amazon Forest down there. This guy is clearly not into manscaping, but I'm about to change that. After my shower, I change into a pair of sweatpants and a T-shirt 'cause I can't find any of his PJs. Then I crawl back into bed. There's a soft knock on the door, and the lady who brought me here walks in.

"How are you feeling, Kobe?"

"I've been better, to be honest."

Don't worry, dear; I've spoken to Mr Calhoon. You are more than welcome to return to school on Monday. And as for that Mr Fairview, his days at your school are numbered."

I don't know what to say to that, so I shrug in compliance.

"Oh, and your father wishes you well. He wanted to check in on you, but he is knackered. He turned in early. You should get some rest, too. Good night, Kobe."

"Good night, Mum."

Kobe Dewinter

As I'm jogging down the street, I try to come up with a plan. So far, I know that I'm in another dude's body – Jai's, to be exact. I have two dads, and Jai is as camp as Christmas. My dads are seriously invested in my well-being, but I can't afford to let them take me to a doctor. If they find out I'm not who they think I am, I might end up in an asylum. I have to get as much intel as I can about this place so I can plan my next move. I finally have a lucky break 'cause Jai's phone unlocks with a fingerprint.

I scroll through Jai's missed calls. There are about two dozen from Josh and one from Jaimy. Most of his text messages are from two chicks called Selma and Jess. They're obsessed with Jai because they keep begging him to call them or let them know how he's doing. At the end of the street, I turn left. A woman shushing a high-strung beagle in her garden waves at me to come over.

"Jai, honey, I'm so glad to see you on your feet again. You gave me and Laura quite a fright yesterday when we found you in the park. I've been telling people at our town gatherings to shut that bridge down ages ago. This was an accident waiting to happen."

I suddenly come up with an idea: maybe this is not the first time this has happened, and maybe there are others like me wandering around town.

"Uhm, do you know if a fall like mine has happened before?"

"Oh goodness no, we're usually very meticulous about maintenance in this town. Although Mr Hubert fell down a ladder last year while cleaning the gutter. That was on him, though; he shouldn't have gone up there in the first place with his arthritis. It took his poor husband months to nurse him back to health."

"Thanks, Mrs…"

"Oh, do call me Ann, darling; we've known each other for ages."

"Thanks, Ann. I need to be going now. Say hi to Laura from me."

"I will love, glad to see you in one piece."

Great! So far, I've learned nothing new except that there are quite a few queers on the block. As I ponder my next step, I hear my name. As I turn around, I see two girls heading my way. One of the girls slams into me and gives me a big bear hug.

"Jai, oh my God, we've been so worried. Why didn't you text us? How are you? Are you hurt? I'm so sorry about Josh."

"Jess, come on, give the guy some room to breathe. You're practically crushing the poor man."

"I know, Selma, but I was up half the night worrying about him."

"I know, pumpkin. I didn't get much sleep either, with you texting next to me all night long."

It's my cue to say something.

"Sorry, ladies, I was exhausted yesterday, and my head was still sore. But I'm much better today."

"Jai, I don't know what to say. I'm so sorry about Jaimy and Josh," Selma says sheepishly.

"I hit my head pretty hard, Selma; I can't exactly remember what happened."

"Oh, you poor thing," Jess says while clinging to my arm.

"Well, I hate to break it to you, Jai, but you walked in on your boyfriend Josh making out with my brother Jaimy."

"Right, I see. That really sucks."

"Can't believe I didn't notice something was going on between those two," Selma says. "I'm furious with my brother, and Mum and Dad aren't too pleased either. Jaimy knows he screwed up pretty badly, but he's crazy about Josh."

Jess wraps her arms around me.

"You know, Jai, those jerks deserve each other. You're the best, and you will find true love."

"Thanks; you guys are great."

"We know," Selma says, giving me a small wink.

"My awesomeness is why Jess fell head over heels with me."

"Who's being a jerk now," Jess says, but she quickly gives Selma a peck on the lips.

"Ladies, I'd love to chat, but if I stay out longer than half an hour, my dads will organise a search party."

"Of course, Jai, they must have been so worried about you. See you at school then?"

"You sure will."

Selma and Jess take off, holding hands. Holy sh*t, my two best pals are gay too? What is this place? I'm not ready to go home. I might find out more about this town in the library. I'll have to let Vikram and Robin know that I'll be out for a bit longer. I text Robin, I ran into Jess and Selma, and that we're catching up. I get a thumbs-up emoji in reply, so that's settled.

I walk along the road and see a signpost saying Malcolm Michaels Centre. I head in that direction and come across the library on my way. Once I'm in, I have no idea where to look for anything that might clarify where I am. The librarian spots me and walks up to me.

"Good morning, Jai. I've heard you took quite a fall the other day. How are you feeling?"

Wow, news travels fast around here.

"I'm fine, thank you."

"Are you looking for anything in particular? Your friend Jess told me you kids have book reports coming up. Have you got a book yet?"

Oh great, now I'm expected to do homework?

"Uhm, no, ma'am, I haven't."

"Don't worry about it; let me walk you to your favourite section, the classics."

Not surprised, Jai has a nerdy taste in books as well. As not to look suspicious, I pretend to take an interest. I squat down to take a closer look at some of the titles. I spot Romeo & Julius, Tristan & Isaac, and Mr Bingley in a tight embrace with Mr Darcy on the cover of Pride and Prejudice. Wait what?

I'm no expert on the classics; believe me, I tried very hard to avoid them in my literature class last year. But something's definitely off here. I'm pretty sure it's *Romeo & Juliet*, and wasn't Tristan with this chick called Isolde? What about Mr Bingley and Mr Darcy? No way would that go down well in regency England. There must be some sort of mistake, or do they make queer copies of every classic these days? I walk up to the librarian, who is at her desk.

"Uhm, excuse me."

"Yes, Jai, what can I do for you?"

"Well, it's just that section with the classics; they strike me as a bit odd."

"Why is that?"

"I was wondering where you keep the originals?"

"The originals of what?"

"The original scripts of all those queer copies. It's supposed to be Romeo & Juliet, Tristan and Isolde, and Mr Darcy was definitely not courting some dude in regency London."

"Jai, I don't know what you're talking about; we only have original copies at the library."

"Oh, come on, really? Every character in every book's gay now? What the heck?"

"Darling, are you all right? Should I call Vikram or Robin? You seem terribly out of sorts."

Oh no, she can't call my dads.

"Uhm, no, I'm fine. I'm sorry. I guess I just misread some of the titles. I'm really tired; I'm going home."

"Don't you want to check out anything, love?"

"No, thank you. I'll come back another time."

It's definitely time to go home now, 'cause I don't know if I can take much more today.

Jai Patel-Jones

My so-called mum, Mrs Dewinter, drops me off at school on Monday morning. My headache is mostly gone by now. I'm excused from PE today, which suits me just fine. This morning, I was briefly tempted to stay in bed. But if I am to figure out why I'm here and how to get home, I need a better understanding of this place. That will not happen in bed with the sheets pulled up to my chin. Today, I'm dressed in a pair of slim denim jeans and a plain shirt. Not that I had much to choose from in the first place. His wardrobe mainly consists of hoodies, plain shirts and jeans. Nonetheless, these clothes are a snug fit and really bring out my abs and arm muscles. Something I can't get enough of since I never had any of my own. Kobe's timetable is on his phone, which is easy to access since his password is 1234. My first period is arts with Mr Blend. I love arts and crafts; back home, I was working on an ornamental bird feeder in wood shop. When I enter the classroom, Jake and Roy aren't there yet. I skim over all the faces to decide where to sit, when I notice this guy at a table in the back. He has caramel-coloured skin, his eyes are almond-shaped, and he has a pair of glasses perched on a cute button nose. He seems lost in his artwork, trying to fold and glue something at the same time. The tip of his tongue sticks out, and his brows are furrowed in concentration. I don't want to throw him off of whatever he's doing, so I sit down quietly. He finally notices me and looks up at me in surprise.

"Hi," I say as an icebreaker. "What are you working on?"

"Why do you want to know, Kobe? You're looking for anything else to wreck?"

I'm dumbfounded.

"Why would I want to do that?"

"You did a pretty awesome job on those rainbow flags, spray painting phalluses all over them, next to a drawing of my face."

My jaw drops, and I have no idea how to respond to his. Did Kobe seriously do this? What is wrong with him?

The guy continues.

"Or did you hit your head so hard you forgot what a dick you've been and how you've made my life a living hell this past year?"

"Uhm, I hurt my head pretty badly, and to be honest, I can't remember everything that happened," I finally manage to croak out.

"How convenient for you, Kobe. It must be great to get this many do-overs without any accountability."

Oh no, this guy is really upset with me. Then I hear Jake calling.

"Oi, Kobe over here, we've saved you a seat."

I turn around and see Jake and Roy sitting at the front of the class, with one empty seat left. I get up and join them.

"What was all that about with you and Pussyto?" Jake asks.

"Who?"

"Paquito, Kobe, why were you sitting next to him? Or did you give him a heads up on what's in store for him this afternoon?"

"Why would I do that?"

"Try to keep up, Kobe," Roy interrupts. "We added a little extra to all of those hideous rainbow flags last week, and he ratted you out to the principal. He nearly got you expelled."

I sit back and take a deep breath. Then it dawns on me: I'm a bully and a homophobe. The rest of the morning goes by in a haze. I go through the motions and feign interest in whatever we do in class. Jake and Roy keep trying to get me to join in their conversations, but I'm hardly in the mood. If Paquito is right about Kobe, and I have very little reason to doubt him, judging by how Jake and Roy talk about him, I'm the worst person ever.

After the break, I have a free period, which I decide to spend in the school's library. Reading a classic will take my mind off things and hopefully give me a little break from all the madness around me. I head straight for the Shakespeare shelf; a good old love story like Rome & Julius is just what I need right now. That's weird, there's definitely a copy of the play I'm looking for, but it's called *Romeo & Juliet*. Why would they put Romeo's sister in the title rather than Julius, the love of his life? Must be an alternative love story. I'll ask the librarian for an original copy. Just as I'm about to head to her desk, I spot Paquito. He's engrossed in a comic, laughing quietly to himself. His dark curls dance around his face every time he chuckles. I walk up to him.

"Sorry to disturb you, but can I have a minute of your time?"

"What do you want now, Kobe?"

"It's just that I think we got off on the wrong foot this morning. As I understand it, I've been horrible to you, and I just want you to know how sorry I am. I'm sorry for spray painting those flags, and I'm sorry for everything else I've done this year to upset you."

"How hard did you hit your head, Kobe? You're never sorry about anything. Or is this one of those pranks you and your cronies have come up with?"

"I don't know what else to say, Paquito. I can't undo what

Kobe, Uhm, what I did to you. I just want you to know I'm deeply sorry, and it won't happen again."

"What a lovely speech, Kobe, if only I had any reason to take your word for it. Which I don't, so please leave."

I take one more look at the boy I've damaged beyond repair and walk out of the library. I'm fighting back tears as I head to my next class. I'm an awful person with awful friends in a place that feels completely alien to me. My only light in the dark is Paquito, a boy who hates me.

Kobe Dewinter

"How are Selma and Jess doing, Jai? Did you guys have a nice chat?"

Ever since I've been back home Vikram and Robin are firing questions at me like the Spanish Inquisition. "I'll bet Selma feels awful about Jaimy and Josh; Mrs Murphy is livid with her son," Robin says.

"Have you talked to Josh yet? Has Jaimy reached out at all? If you need a little more time to process what has happened, you can stay home on Monday," Vikram tells me.

"I'll work from home, so I can take care of you, darling," Robin adds.

Staying home is not going to solve anything, so I declined their offer. I appreciate their concern and willingness to put everything on hold just to be there for me. No one's ever done that for me or even considered doing so. Truth be told, it's a bit suffocating too. I understand Jai's life isn't exactly a walk in the park right now, but he has nothing to be ashamed of. I'll go to school on Monday and show them what I'm made of.

Jess walks me to my locker before the first period. Just as well, because I have no idea where it is. I hover in front of it since I don't know my locker combination. Thankfully, Jess is there to help out.

"It's your birthday silly, which is on 5 October, you're a Libra. Your locker combination is 510."

"Oh, great, thanks, Jess. I'll catch up with you in class."

I open Jai's locker to get my books for the first period. Holy hell, it's basically a shrine in here. There are pictures of Josh and Jai cello-taped to every inch of the surface available. Most pictures are decorated with little rhinestones and colourful hearts, and there's even a LED-powered tea light perched on a small treasure chest filled with tokens of their previous dates. A cinema ticket, a receipt for coffee and scones, a heart-shaped rock, and whatnot. I'm about to close my locker when I hear feet shuffle behind me. I turn around to see Josh, at least that's the guy I recognise from all the pictures.

"Jai, I've been so worried about you. Why haven't you answered any of my calls?"

"Oh, that's how it is now. Do I have to answer to you?"

I don't know why, but I suddenly feel a lot of resentment towards this guy who screwed Jai over.

"I'm so sorry about what happened. Can we meet after school to talk about it?"

"I'm not sure I see the point of that."

"Oh, Jai, don't be like that; this isn't you."

"Well, maybe it's the new me since you've ignored and neglected me and hooked up with someone else. I don't know what I did to deserve this, but I'm not sure I'm even interested in finding out any more."

On the spur of the moment, I open my locker again and start tearing off every picture covering the inside. I grab the treasure chest and tea light and head for the nearest bin. I dump all that I can carry and slam the door of my locker shut.

"See, Josh, I've moved on; perhaps you should too."

Josh stares at me open-mouthed.

I'm about to head to class when I hear someone slow-clap

behind me. I turn around to see a petit brunette smiling up at me. She's wearing baggy jeans, a Grateful Dead shirt and army-style boots. The lower tips of her hair are dyed bright pink. I've no idea who this is.

"Uh, thank you?" I hesitantly say.

"Well done. Josh really had that coming. I can't believe the crap he and Jaimy pulled on you."

"Right, I'm not too happy about it either, but as far as I'm concerned, that dude is no longer part of my life. Uhm, have we met before?"

"We have, but Selma told me you hit your head pretty hard. I'm Lexi. We're in Homeroom together."

"Great, well, nice to meet you again, Lexi."

"Listen, Jai, if you ever need someone to talk to, just let me know, okay?"

"Well, I do suffer from a bit of memory loss. Can I pick your brain after school?"

"Sure, no problem. Talk to you then."

First period hasn't even started yet, but I feel I could use a break after all the drama. That Lexi girl seemed really nice, though, and maybe she can shed some light on this place.

Jai Patel-Jones

Time flies when you're having fun, which is not the case today. Time has slowed to a crawl, probably because I'm feeling miserable. I've been trying to avoid Jake and Roy, using lots of homework to catch up with as an excuse. Truth is, they're both toxic. They're bullies just like Kobe, and the three of them have made Paquito's life dreadful this year. I don't even know where to start cleaning up this mess, and I seriously doubt that's even possible. On top of that I haven't got a clue how to get back home to my dads. After the last period, I call Kobe's mum. She's agreed to pick me up after school. I'm waiting for her near the school's bike shed. I've managed to dodge Jake and Roy all day, so when I hear their voices, I hide.

"Are you sure that little fag, Paquito, will be here soon?"

"School's out, Jake.–His bike is right over there. Too bad Kobe isn't here with us. He would have loved this."

"I've no idea where he's at; he's been acting strange all day. He even seemed upset when I mentioned we had something in store for Pussyto this afternoon."

"Well, it's his loss. He's missing out on all the fun, Jake."

Oh no, they're going after Paquito! I have to warn him. But I am too late, because there he is. Most students have left; his bike is the only one left in the shed. Jake and Roy can do to him whatever they want. Paquito enters the shed and starts unlocking his bike. Then Jake and Roy appear.

"Oi, Pussyto, not so fast; where are you off to?"

"None of your business, Jake; leave me alone."

"Why would we do that?" Roy adds. "You almost got Kobe expelled, and we lost an important game, 'cause he was stuck in detention last Saturday."

"Serves him right; he should leave school property alone."

"Well, aren't you a little saint, Pussyto? But it's your lucky day because we happen to have some of that spray paint left. Let's see if we can brighten up that atrocious face of yours."

"Try spelling 'atrocious', Roy; don't use big words you can't write."

Roy's face turns red as he lunges at Paquito, spray paint ready. Paquito ducks, but Jake is there to hold him down. I can't let this happen.

"Hey, Roy, leave him alone. Give it a rest, Jake!" I shout at them.

"Kobe, what are you doing here? Come to enjoy the show?"

"This isn't funny, Roy; let him go; what has he ever done to you?"

"Since when do you care, Kobe? Last week, you were all up in his face, just like us."

"I know, and that was horrible. I don't want to be like that any more."

"Oh, so now you're a saint too? At least don't get in our way," Jake snarls.

I grab Kobe's phone and switch it to camera.

"I'm filming this; if you don't let him go, I'll show everyone what you did to him, including Mr Calhoon."

"Oh, now you're a grass, Kobe? Real nice."

Both Jake and Roy realise I'm ready to put my money where my mouth is. They finally back off. Before they're out of sight, Jake turns around.

"You can find yourself some new friends to hang out with, Kobe; we're done."

Paquito is standing next to his bike, visibly shaken.

"Are you all right?"

"No, I am not, seeing as those mates of yours just terrorised me."

"They're not my friends any more, and in case you haven't noticed, I stopped them."

"Oh, thanks a lot, Kobe. Doing the right thing for once doesn't make you a hero. And it doesn't make up for all those times you didn't stick up for me."

Before I can say anything else, he jumps on his bike and leaves. I'm so sick of it. Whatever I do, I can't seem to get it right. I've never felt lonelier in my life. When my ride arrives, tears are streaming down my face. I get in the car. Kobe's mum drives off, blatantly ignoring how upset I am.

Kobe Dewinter

I spent my lunchbreak with Selma and Jess. Jess is really excited about their upcoming swim meet. They're both on the school's swim team, and they're competing against last year's regional champion. "You have to come and cheer us on, Jai," Selma says. "It's this Saturday, and we need all the support we can get."

"Thanks for the invite, but I don't know if Vikram and Robin have anything planned for this weekend. I'll let you know, okay?"

"You do that, Jai; feel free to bring your dads along if you want to," Jess adds.

My dads, it feels strange to hear those words, let alone use them myself. If anyone had told me a week ago that I'd live with two dads, I would have called them insane. And I'd been disgusted, too. My parents are quite traditional and have never encouraged me to think outside of the box.

As far as they know, any worthwhile relationship or marriage consists of a man and a woman, or a husband and wife. Same-sex relationships are a bunch of woke nonsense, and people really need to snap out of it, my dad claims. If he knew I was being raised by two men, he'd been repulsed. In the short time I've been here, I've come to know Vikram and Robin as generous, caring, and dedicated dads. It baffles me how much they love Jai and would do anything to make him happy and keep him safe. It's in sharp contrast with the relationship I have with my parents. Of course, they love me, it's just that they hardly ever show. They're so absorbed by their work and their separate career paths that they've lost track of each other as a couple and of me as their son. And I act out because it's the only way to get their attention. I think back to all those times I've been up to no good with my sidekicks, Jake and Roy. This queer kid, Paquito, has mostly been on the receiving end of our banter and pranks. Something he never asked for or deserved. It makes me blush when I think of how we treated him. Always three against one, and for what?

To blow off steam, picking on a kid who wouldn't fight back. If I ever get the chance, I'll apologise and tell him it's not okay what I did. I have no idea if I'll ever be able to do that. I can't just pick up the phone and give him a call. But wait, Jai has a working cell phone; what if I use his phone to send a message to mine? It sounds so crazy that it might just work. If I'm in Jai's body, then he's probably in mine, living my life. Oh crap, a queer boy is going to my school, flanked by dudes like Jake and Roy. Staying at my house with my not-very-accepting parents. I hope he's okay. All I can think of typing is:

Hey, it's me, Kobe.
I hope you're all right, Jai.
If you get this message, please let me know.

I press send and wait. 'Message not received', I read. Just my luck, I'm cut off from my world and Jai from his.

"Hey, Jai, wait up."

I turn around, and there's Lexi. She runs up to me, slightly out of breath.

"I thought that was you, absorbed by your phone. Who're you texting, hope it's not Josh?"

"No, of course not, kicked his ass to the curb this morning, didn't I?"

"You sure did, Jai. You said you wanted to speak to me."

"Uhm, yes, it's just that I'm having a hard time picking up where I left off. I feel like a stranger in my own skin. Doesn't help that I seem to have forgotten so much basic stuff about my own life."

"Have you talked to your dads about this?"

"No. Not really; don't want them to worry about me or drag me to the hospital."

"Yep, that sounds exactly like something Vikram and Robin would do."

"So I thought; perhaps you could give me the lay of the land, so to speak."

"Fire away, hon."

"First of all, and I hope this doesn't sound weird, but everyone seems queer in his town."

"What do you mean by queer, Jai?"

"Well, most people are in a same-sex relationship or marriage."

"What about it, Jai?"

"Suppose nothing, but aren't there any straight people in town?"

"What do you mean by that?"

"Any *normal* relationship between a boy and girl or husband and wife."

"Any relationship based on love, consent, and mutual respect *is* normal. But to answer your question, there aren't many straight couples in town. Come to think of it, my parents are the only ones I know of."

"Your parents are straight?"

"Yes, Mum and Dad met in college; it was love at first sight. Couldn't wait to tie the knot after graduation."

"Don't they ever feel like outsiders?"

"Nope, as far as they and everyone else in this town are concerned, love is love. They're part of this community just like everyone else." By the way, would you like to go to the school's swim meet with me this Saturday? That is, if your dads haven't carted you off to the ICU by tomorrow morning."

"Sounds great, Lexi."

"Cool, my brother and his girlfriend are coming too."

"Your brother has a girlfriend?"

"Well, he's dated this guy Marty for nearly a year, but they broke up last summer. He's into Lisa now; they make a cute couple."

"Nice. It's a date, then."

"A date?"

"Uhm, that's not what I meant; I was…"

"Just messing with you, Jai; see you on Saturday. I'll text you when and where."

Lexi takes off on a run. She turns around to give me a final wave, but then she's out of sight. Suppose not everything down here is a total disaster.

Jai Patel-Jones

Back home, I head straight for my room. I'm in no mood to talk to anyone. I scroll through Kobe's messages. There's one from Coach Bates reminding Kobe to come early to tonight's soccer practice. Other than that, nobody seems to have reached out. I miss going over my own texts. After school, Selma, Jess and I would FaceTime. We'd talk about Stonewall High's latest hookups and breakups, upcoming sports events, or the play my boyfriend is co-directing. I wonder if Josh ever thinks about me and if he regrets his affair with Jaimy and is now tearfully awaiting my return. But what if I never really left? If I'm here in Kobe's body, wouldn't it make sense that he's over there in mine? This means that I'm technically still there, only an entirely different version of myself. What I've learned so far about Kobe is not very reassuring. My town is stuck with a homophobic teen, a bully who goes to extremes to make others feel miserable. I start typing a message, delete it, and then type it again. Before I can change my mind, I press send. Don't know if it will make a difference, but at least I've tried.

My dad's calling me to come downstairs.

"Kobe, you have soccer practice. I'll drive you there; hurry up, or you'll be late."

Soccer practice? I hate ball games. I couldn't kick a ball if I sat on it.

"Dad, I think I won't go; still feeling a bit under the weather."

"Nonsense, Kobe, walk it off; don't be such a pansy, son."

Three minutes later, I'm in the car on my way to my first soccer practice. Coach Bates pulls me aside as soon as he sees me.

"Kobe, we missed you at the game last Saturday; it would have been an easy win if you had been there. No use crying over spilt milk, though. If we bag this Saturday's match, the title is ours."

I don't know what to say because I'm pretty sure I'd be useless on the pitch. We start our practice by doing warming-up exercises. I'm relieved I can keep up with the rest. Jake and Roy are here too, but they barely acknowledge my presence. After we've warmed up, we take turns taking penalties. I miss each and every one of them. One shot is so far off that it takes me a while to retrieve the ball. Then we're split into two groups, playing a proper match. Jake and Roy are on the other team. Coach Bates keeps yelling at me.

"What are you doing back there, Kobe? You're a striker. Come on, move, run and go after that ball dammit!"

He finally gives it a rest, mainly because I won't go past the centre line. Bates is definitely not pleased with me; he lets me stay behind to store away all the equipment. By the time I get to hit the showers, most of my teammates have left. After I've changed, I leave for the parking lot, where my dad's waiting to pick me up.

"Kobe, wait."

"Yes, Coach?"

"I don't know what's up with you today, but I hope I'll never see such an abysmal performance again."

"Sorry, Coach, I guess I'm still a bit out of sorts."

"Well, Kobe, you better get it together soon 'cause we need

you to be at your best this Saturday."

"Yes, Coach."

I walk up to the car, one hundred per cent sure that this is my first and last soccer practice. Come hell or high water, I won't be on that pitch on Saturday.

Early the next morning, I pick a seat at the back of the class. The teacher is setting up for today's history lesson. Thankfully, the rest of my class hasn't arrived yet. Most of my classmates avoid me like the plague. They're either on team Jake & Roy, or team Paquito, and I haven't got a fan base for either of them. When my classmates start pouring in, they steal brief glances at me, wondering who will eventually sit down next to me. The so-called lucky winner is Yousef. A shy kid who nods when people address him and mostly keeps to himself. Our teacher sets out an assignment for us to hand in by next week. We have to pair up and write a paper. Poor Yousef; it looks like he's stuck with me. The teacher announces the topic: unsung heroes. We're free to narrow it down and pick whoever we want. Our teacher explains that heroes and villains are easy to come by when reading about history. But what about those who did good deeds, made a difference in people's lives, and never got the recognition they deserved? It's our job this week to pick one of those unsung heroes and put them in the spotlight. I have so many ideas that my head's spinning. But I'm doing this paper with Yousef, so we both get an equal say in this.

"So," I start carefully. "Do you have any time to work on the paper this week?"

Yousef looks at me and nods.

"Oh, uhm, great, any thoughts on when?"

"This afternoon."

"Great, shall we meet in the library then?"

"Have to pick up my little brother after school, so maybe at my place?"

"Oh, sure, I'll ask my mum to pick me up there."

Yousef nods in agreement, and that's the end of our spirited conversation.

Kobe Dewinter

I'm in front of the town's sports centre, waiting for Lexi. It's a huge building, and according to the website, it offers all sorts of indoor and outdoor facilities. Luckily, the competition pool is inside since there's been a steady drizzle for a while now. It took me some time to get dressed this morning. I wanted to look nice but not overdressed since it's obviously not a date. Vikram caught up to my nervous vibe and helped me pick out an outfit. I settled for a pair of slim-fit jeans and a burgundy-coloured polo. It surprises me that I've hardly missed my own wardrobe. Baggy jeans and hoodies would have probably looked bad on Jai anyway. Then I spot Lexi, who's wearing her hair in two pigtails tied with black ribbons. Her army-style boots are underneath a knee-length purple skirt, topped by another Grateful Dead shirt.

"Kobe, over here!"

Lexi has spotted me, too.

"Hey, Lexi, how are you?"

"Great, can't wait to get out of this rain, though. Oh, and this is my brother Collin and his girlfriend Lisa."

"Nice to meet you guys."

They do indeed make a cute couple. They're holding hands, fingers intertwined. They are both wearing matching shirts with the swim team's logo on them. We don't waste any more time getting wet, and head inside. Selma and Jess are both competing in the 200-metre butterfly stroke and 400-metre freestyle. When it's their turn, Lexi is so nervous that she clings to my arm for support. I'm only too happy to return the favour and hold her as tight as any platonic friendship would allow. We cheer them on as loud as we can, and it pays off. Selma wins the 200-metre butterfly stroke, and Jess is runner-up in the 400-metre freestyle. We're all in the mood to celebrate. However, Selma and Jess have a celebratory lunch with their swim team and, Lisa is taking Collin to her gran's birthday party. So, in the end, it's just me and Lexi.

"Want to come over to my place? My dad's baked scones, and we have some of Mum's homemade blackberry jam left."

"That's an offer I can't refuse."

We both laugh and walk to Lexi's bike.

"You can hop on if you like, Jai."

Jai's petit figure could easily fit on the luggage carrier, but I'd rather be the one pedalling. So, I end up cycling while Lexi sits in the back, her arms wrapped around my waist.

Lexi's parents are out on their weekly trip to the farmers' market. They left some delicious-smelling scones on the kitchen counter with a generous helping of blackberry jam. We help ourselves and sit down to eat.

"So, Jai, are you starting to feel a little more like yourself again?"

"I'm getting there, Lexi; it really helps having you there to fill in the blanks."

"Glad, I can help Jai. How are you catching up with your schoolwork?"

"I have a book report due next week, haven't started yet."

"Really? You love reading, especially the classics. Remember when Mr Lewis forgot to assign us our midterm book report, you vigorously reminded him. The entire class didn't speak to you for a week."

"Wow, I landed myself and everyone else extra homework? Surprised I have any friends left."

"Well, apart from your overzealousness concerning literature, you're quite a likeable guy, Jai."

"Thanks, Lexi. I went to the library the other day, but nothing looked familiar to me."

"Why don't you pick Shakespeare's Romeo & Julius? You practically know it by heart."

"About that, Lexi, I remember that story a bit differently. Why is it called Romeo and Julius instead of Romeo and Juliet?"

"Because Romeo and Julius are the main characters. They fall madly in love with each other, despite their rivalling families."

"Yeah, but wouldn't it make more sense if Romeo ended up with Juliet?"

"Why on earth would Romeo want to end up with his sister?"

"Wait, what? Juliet is his sister?"

"Yes, she helps her brother and Julius get together and sets up their escape plan. Of course, it all ends rather tragically, but it's still a great love story."

I stare at Lexi open-mouthed. *Holy crap*, the greatest love story of all time is queer.

"Look, Jai, don't worry, I'll lend you my copy. I'm sure it will all come back to you."

My phone starts buzzing, and I see a text from Robin reminding me I have a class at the gym this afternoon. Good, Jai's into working out. Could use a bit of exercise. A spinning class would be very welcome or maybe even a power pump class. Can't wait to lift some weights, do some crunches, and work on my abs.

"Thanks for the scones, Lexi, but I need to get going.

Heading for the gym this afternoon."

"You're welcome, Jai. Have fun at your workout."

Lexi tries to suppress a giggle when she says that, which strikes me as odd. Maybe she thinks Jai isn't in shape, but I'll prove her wrong.

Jai Patel-Jones

After we pick up his brother Haroon from primary school, we walk over to Yousef's place. We settle down in his living room while Haroon is outside playing soccer with the neighbourhood kids. We can hear their shrieks and laughter as they call each other by their favourite players.

"Over here, Ronaldo. I'm free." We hear Haroon call.

"Come on, Messi, pass the ball," someone else shouts.

Yousef gets us a coke from the fridge and settles down next to me on the couch.

"You play too, don't you?" he asks.

"Not any more if it's up to me. I think I've outgrown the game."

"Is it because you fell out with Jake and Roy?"

"That sure didn't help. But truth be told, I'd rather be doing something else with my time."

"Well, for now, we've got a paper to write, Kobe. Any idea which hero we should choose?"

"Actually, I do have an idea. How about Bayard Rustin? He was an all-round civil rights activist who campaigned for gay rights too."

"That's a great idea; I heard about him in history class. Wasn't he the deputy director of the March on Washington and close adviser to Martin Luther King? After his death, Barack Obama awarded him with the Presidential Medal of Freedom."

"That's the one, Yousef. After the march, he changed his

focus to gay rights. One of the many things he achieved is getting the AIDS crisis formally acknowledged by the National Association for the Advancement of Coloured People."

"Sounds like we got ourselves a hero then."

We get to work until Yousef's mum and dad come home.

"Hi, Kobe. Yousef texted us that you were coming over to work on a school project. Nice to meet you. I'm Saida, and this is my husband, Achmed. Would you like to stay for dinner?"

"Uhm, I guess so, if it's not too much trouble. I'll ask my mum to pick me up around eight."

"Do you like Manakeesh and Tabbouleh, Kobe?"

"I've never had it before, but it sounds delicious, Mrs Khan."

And it sure is. Mrs Khan is an amazing cook. I keep telling Yousef how lucky he is. Kobe's parents are not really into cooking. They order takeout on most days, or forget to have dinner altogether when they're absorbed by their jobs. Luckily, their fridge is abundantly stocked, so I never go hungry. But it's been a while since I've had a proper sit-down family meal. The Khans are a lovely family, laughing and teasing each other while sharing how their day was. Yousef is much more talkative around his family than he is at school. He really seems at ease with them. I'm happy he's got such a lovely home. It reminds me of my own home with Vikram and Robin.

I miss them so much, but that won't bring them back. I also believe in destiny. If I'm here in Kobe's place, the universe must have had its reasons for putting me there. And when I'm done doing whatever I'm supposed to do here, I have no doubt I'll find my way back somehow.

After dinner, we have some time left before my mum picks me up. We go up to Yousef's room, which he shares with his brother. One half is littered with toys and Pokémon cards; the other half is neatly organised. Yousef has his schoolbooks stacked on one side of his desk, while his stationery is carefully placed on the other side. If it weren't for the pictures on the wall, it could have very well been an office space. Luckily, Troye Sivan's looking up at me from a movie poster for Spud 4. Then I spot another one.

"Oh my God, Yousef, I have the same poster of Timothée Chalamet on my wall. Doesn't he look great in that outfit?"

Yousef blushes and looks at me weirdly.

Oh no, I forgot. Jai has a poster of him, but Kobe obviously doesn't.

"Uhm, I mean, I've seen that poster somewhere else before. But it's nice, though."

"So, you don't think it's weird?"

"Why would I think that, Yousef? It's a great pic. Why should it matter who's on your wall anyway? You're free to like whoever you want."

"Surprised to hear you say that, Kobe; you've got quite a nasty rep when it comes down to accepting anything that is not right up your street."

"I know I've been a downright twat for the past year, Yousef. I'm not proud of it. In fact, I'm horrified at how I behaved. I'm trying to make amends and better my life. That's why I fell out with Jake and Roy; they're still stuck in their old ways. Most people at school haven't received the memo about the new me yet, so that's why people avoid me like a disgraced televangelist."

"I'm sorry to hear that, Kobe; I believe you've changed. That's why I sat down next to you in history class. You were giving off a different vibe than before – one I actually liked. And it helped that Paquito told me you stood up for him the other day when he was being harassed by Jake and Roy."

"Wait, what? Paquito talked about me?"

"Yeah, he couldn't believe his eyes when you took your mates on to defend him. You even threatened to tell on them."

"I thought he wasn't very impressed with me. He barely acknowledged what I did."

"Can you blame him, Kobe? You've bullied him all year long. No wonder he has some trust issues."

"Since when are you friends with Paquito?"

"We're both in the GSA at school."

"The GSA?"

"Gender-Sexuality-Alliance. We're a group of queer and straight teens passionate about inclusion, especially when it comes to LGBTQ+ rights. We organise events such as those Purple Fridays."

"That sounds great, Yousef."

"Would you like to come to our next meeting?"

"Are they even going to want me there after all that's happened?"

"I'll talk to them, Kobe, and let you know."

"Thanks, Yousef."

Then my phone buzzes to let me know my mum is waiting for me.

Kobe Dewinter

When I get home, Robin has already packed my gym bag.

"Hurry up; love, your class is in ten minutes. You know that David hates starting without you."

"Okay, but what class am I in exactly?"

"David's class, darling, now get in the car. I'll drop you off."

Five minutes later, we're at the gym.

"Everything you need's in the bag, love. Tell David I said hi. I'll pick you up in an hour."

"Will do, Dad. See you."

I walk inside and head for the locker room. I open my gym bag to find a towel, a water bottle, body wash, a pair of indoor sneakers, and my outfit. There must have been some sort of mix-up, because all I find is a pair of bright yellow leggings and a matching top with the word 'fierce' spelled in silver-coloured sequins. Who on earth would anyone wear this while indoor cycling or lifting weights? I'm about to call Robin when a sports instructor enters.

"Hey, Jai, so good to have you with us again today. Robin texted me you were coming."

Oh, so this must be David. He's wearing an outfit similar to the one I just found in my bag. A pair of turquoise leggings and a pink top with a floral print. In addition, he's wearing legwarmers and a headband.

"I think Robin packed me the wrong outfit."

David takes one look at my brightly coloured leggings and

top.

"That's what you're always wearing, silly, now chop-chop. Everyone else is already here."

David isn't leaving, so I have no choice but to change into this ridiculous outfit and follow him into the gym. There's a group of about fifteen other dudes waiting for us, all in colourful leggings and tops. David walks over to a sound installation in the corner of the room. He puts on a headset with a mike and walks up to the front.

"Okay, people, let's warm up those muscles, shall we? And five-six-seven-eight."

The music begins, and everyone starts marching to the beat. In the beginning, it's just a left-right-left step in place, but then we start waving our arms as well. I feel absolutely preposterous doing aerobics in an outfit that is more campy than I can handle.

After warming up, I still harbour some hope of finally lifting weights. But no, the aerobics workout intensifies when step planks are introduced. I'd like to think that I'm in quite decent shape, but I can't keep up with the rhythm while attempting an intricate choreography using a step plank. It doesn't help that David decides to do a little one-on-one coaching. He is shouting instructions at me through the mike on his headset.

"Come on, Jai, left-right-left, now turn around and step-step. Don't forget your arms, Jai."

I'm about to collapse when David announces a short break. I lunge for my water bottle and towel. I'm soaked in sweat and out of breath. Everyone around me seems to be just fine.

No one's even broken a sweat. I haul myself up when I see Lexi peering through a window. Oh no, what is she doing here? She spots me, too, and waves. I've already decided I'm not doing another round of aerobics, so I leave the room. Lexi walks up to me. I try to keep my distance, 'cause, boy, do I smell!

"I thought I saw you there doing step aerobics, Jai."

"Great, but what are you doing here, Lexi?"

"I'm picking up Collin from yoga. His car broke down, and I offered to drive him home. How's your class, Jai? You seem a bit flustered."

"To be honest, Lexi, I don't think it's my thing any more. I can't keep up with all the steps, and wave my arms to the beat at the same time. I thought I'd be lifting weights or doing some cardio on an indoor bike. I'm calling it a day."

"If you want, I can drop you off; Collin's class is about to finish."

"Thanks, Lexi; that'll be great. Let me take a quick shower. The way I smell, I cannot be around people within three feet."

"Sure, we'll be waiting in the cafeteria."

I head for the locker room and text Robin that I'm hitching a ride with Lexi. Then I hit the showers. While I'm soaping up, I contemplate Jai's life. Although this aerobics class isn't exactly my cup of tea, our lives aren't that different.

We both have families we care about, friends, hobbies, and some high school drama. I wonder how he's coping with the challenges in my life. After I'm dressed, I walk up to the cafeteria. Lexi is having a fruit smoothie, and Collin is sipping chamomile tea.

"Would you like anything, Jai?"

"No thanks, Lexi; I'm good. Hi, Collin, how are you?"

"Hi, Jai, I'm fine. Had a really rewarding class today. I finally got the hang of that downward-facing dog position. You should try yoga sometimes, Jai; it's so relaxing."

"Thanks for the tip, Collin."

There's no way I'm going to manoeuvre myself into any more awkward positions – at least not in public with an audience, that is.

Jai Patel-Jones

This afternoon, I'm having my first GSA meeting. Yousef texted me that I'm welcome to join them. I am a bit nervous, though. Not just because I'll be the new guy. Sadly, my reputation has preceded me, and so far, it's not been an impressive one. Today's silver lining is that I've managed to make a friend. Yousef and I sit together in class now, which takes some of the heat off me. Jake and Roy are still studiously ignoring me, but that doesn't bother me any more. I'm looking forward to this afternoon, and to showing people a different side of me.

"Hey, Kobe, welcome. Take a seat."

Mr Blend, our art teacher who oversees the meetings, is standing at the door.

"Thank you, Mr Blend."

I look around for an empty seat. The one next to Yousef is already taken, so I sit down next to Paquito. Everyone is chatting while surreptitiously stealing glances at me. I get it; I'm the odd one out. I can only hope to earn their trust one day.

"Everyone, settle down, please. Let's start today's meeting. We have lots to discuss."

Once everyone has quieted down, Mr Blend takes out his glasses and peers at a piece of paper in front of him.

"Right. Are we set for that Amnesty International Campaign you were talking about last time, Ben?"

"Yes, sir, we are."

"Perhaps you can fill Kobe in on what it is about."

"Of course, Amnesty International is currently campaigning

for Mahmood Abadi and Ibrahim Aziz. These men were arrested and imprisoned on charges of homosexuality, which is punishable by law in Iran. There are several scenarios concerning their conviction, and none look particularly good. In the worst case, they'll be sentenced to death."

I'm horrified, and that's an understatement. They send people to prison for being gay? And possibly execute them? I nod, since I'm too stunned to speak. Ben continues.

"It gets worse; Abadi's and Aziz's lawyers haven't been in touch with them in weeks for no clear reason. It looks like they are currently denied any legal aid. Since prisons over there are notorious for lack of food, clean water, medical aid and safety in general, we fear for their health and well-being."

"So, what are our immediate points of action, Ben?" Mr Blend asks.

"We are trying to get as many people as possible to sign a petition, which we will then hand to the Iranian embassy. Hopefully, it will encourage them to take action. In addition, we are writing to our local representatives in parliament to bring this to their attention. Furthermore, we'll set up a fundraiser to pay for legal fees or simply to bribe the authorities. Money goes a long way over there; they might let them see their lawyers again."

"Any questions so far, Kobe?" Mr Blend asks.

I shake my head. I'm still processing what I've just learned. We split into groups to discuss how we'll go about our action points.

Everyone seems equally committed to doing whatever we can to help these men.

For the last ten minutes or so, we talk about our next Purple Friday. Kelly is in charge of the GSA's budget.

"Well, we seem to have enough budget left to see us through this year, although, bear in mind we need to buy some new flags. Quite a few of them were defaced during our last Purple Friday."

I turn a bright shade of red. That's my fault – well, Kobe's fault, to be honest. But that won't make a difference here; as far as they know, I'm Kobe. I open my mouth and stammer.

"Uhm, I will pay for those flags since I'm the one responsible for what happened to them. And I'd like to apologise for what I did. It was awful and immature, and I couldn't be more ashamed."

I look at Paquito, and I am close to tears now.

"I'm so sorry, Paquito, for those flags and all the times I made your life hell this year. I wish I could turn back time, but obviously, I can't. I'll do anything I can to show you I'm not that guy any more."

Paquito nods but doesn't say I'm forgiven. It's not his job to redeem me.

Kobe Dewinter

After Lexi drops me off, I head straight for my room. I'm exhausted. I hear Robin stumble up the stairs. Then he stops at my door.

"Thought I heard you come in, Jai. How was your class? I'll bet David was happy to see you again."

"He sure was, Dad. But I don't think I'll be going back there. I didn't have as much fun as I used to."

"Why, what happened? You're great at step aerobics, remember when we went shopping for an outfit? You fell in love with that yellow halter top the second you saw it. You started sewing on those silver-coloured sequins right after we got home. You felt invincible and fierce, just like it says on your top."

"I know, Dad, it's just that lately I've been developing other interests as well. Maybe I'd like to try a sport that is more competitive, like a ball game or something."

"Well, Stonewall High has a very impressive handball team, Jai. And they're having try-outs next week since Josh quit the team."

"Josh quit the team?"

"He's too preoccupied with the play and wants all of his focus to go into co-directing it successfully."

"I'll bet most of that focus will be on Jaimy. Not that I care any more; I've moved on."

"I'm proud of you, Jai; you will fall in love again. And that special someone might be closer by than you think."

I can't help but think of Lexi. She's kind, lively, smart and awesome-looking. I have no idea what she makes of me, though. And then there's that thing where nearly everyone seems to be in a same-sex relationship. I have no idea what her deal is. Not that it's important, since I'm happy to have her as my friend. Before I turn in, I text Lexi to tell her I'm signing up for handball try-outs next week. She texts me a big smiley emoji, a purple heart, a thump up and a puppy face. Looks like I've got her blessing.

I spend most of Saturday working on my book report, using Lexi's copy of *Romeo and Julius*. We read the story in literature class last year, and I've seen the DiCaprio-Danes movie version. And it is nothing like the film or what I've read before. Most of the characters in the story are queer. Romeo has two dads, and Julius has two mums. Juliet is Romeo's sister and has a fling with Paris, a young countess. After a fight with Tybalt, Mercutio dies in Benvolio's arms, who happens to be his long-time lover. I actually like this version better; it seems more passionate than the version I knew. Those Montagues and Capulets really take their queer drama to the next level.

After I'm finished, I go downstairs for a bite to eat. Vikram and Robin are bickering in the garden over where to put the petunias and roses.

"Jai darling, there're leftovers from Saturday's brunch in the fridge. Help yourself; the quiche and gazpacho are really good." Vikram yells.

"Yes, love, your dad and I aren't quite finished yet," Robin adds.

"Well, I'm rather finished with your shenanigans, Robin; this isn't a war of the roses. Just put them wherever you like, then."

"Fine, I might just do that, Vikram."

Before I can witness any more of their back-and-forth, I go inside. The quiche is really delicious, and I savour every bite.

On Sunday morning, I wake up to the smell of freshly baked bread, eggs and bacon. I walk downstairs, where Robin is baking blueberry muffins.

"These are for today's Kiki, Jai. Another batch of my signature muffins."

I'm at a loss for what he's talking about.

"Today's Kiki, Dad?"

"Yes, love, go and get ready. We don't want to be late. Your outfit is in the bathroom, Jai."

"Okay, thanks, I guess?"

That's strange; Robin and Vikram never pick out my clothes; we must be going somewhere fancy. After breakfast, I get dressed. I'm wearing a pair of grey chinos, a pink polo and a pair of loafers. Strangely enough, Vikram and Robin are wearing similar colours. We look like the three stooges, but better dressed. Robin takes his blueberry muffins with him, so it's probably an early brunch we're going to. Most of the town seems to be going, too. Everyone greets each other and makes small talk. Then I spot Lexi and her parents walking slightly ahead of us.

"Do you mind, Vikram? I just spotted a friend."

"Oh no, Jai, not at all; we'll see you there."

"Hey there, Lexi, up and about early too, I see."

"Hi, Jai, wouldn't want to miss a Kiki. These are my parents, by the way."

"Nice to meet you, Jai. I'm Annabel Haines, and this is my husband, George."

"Pleased to meet you, Mr and Mrs Haines."

"Oh, just call us Annabel and George, love. Did you enjoy

the scones?"

"Absolutely, Mrs H... Uhm, I mean Annabel. Especially with that blackberry jam."

"I get that from the farmers market every week, but we tell people it's homemade."

"Your secret's safe with me, Annabel." I laugh.

I walk a little ahead of them with Lexi.

"Your parents are so nice, Lexi."

"Thanks, Jai, kind of like Vikram and Robin, I suppose."

"Without the bickering, that is," I say.

"Oh, you should have heard them this morning, complete mayhem."

"Parents, right? Where's your brother, by the way?"

"Collin stayed over at Lisa's last night; he's coming with them."

"Sounds like they're really close."

"Tell me about it; they're practically engaged. It's a bit creepy, to be honest. But Collin had it real bad after his breakup with Marty, so I guess I'm glad he's happy again."

"What about you, Lexi?"

"What about me, Jai?"

"Anyone special in your life?"

"Oh, I've got plenty of special people in my life, but I'm not romantically involved with any of them, if that's what you mean."

I turn my head away because I can feel myself blush. Luckily, Lexi pretends she doesn't notice.

We walk up to the town hall. Up in bright letters on the front, it says Malcolm Michaels Centre. We're about to walk in when I see a guy being frog-marched up to me by what seems like his mum.

"Moring, Mrs Murphy," Lexi says brightly.

She takes a brief glance at the three of us.

"I'll see you inside, Jai; I'll save you a seat."

It takes a second before it dawns on me. Mrs Murphy is Selma's mum, so this must be Jaimy.

"Hi," I say, staring at them slightly bemused.

"Hello, Jai. Sorry to bother you, but Jaimy would like to say something."

"Okay, what's up, Jaimy?"

"Hi, Jai, uhm, I just wanted to say that I'm sorry that things didn't work out between you and Josh."

"They didn't work out because you kissed him, Jaimy. You kissed my boyfriend."

"Yeah, uhm, I'm sorry about that too."

I'm not about to let him off the hook that easily.

"You're sorry you got caught, or you're sorry you kissed him?"

Jaimy turns a vivid shade of red and shrugs his shoulders. Mrs Murphy is having none of it and slaps the back of his head. Jaimy cringes and looks as if he's about to cry.

"What kind of apology is that, Jaimy? I've raised you better than that."

"I'm sorry, I got between you and Josh. I shouldn't have interfered. That wasn't cool."

"Right, well, thanks for coming over to apologise, Jaimy. It doesn't make what you did any better, but at least you're owning up to it."

With that, I turn around and go inside to look for Lexi.

Jai Patel-Jones

"Well, how did you think it went, Kobe?"

Yousef is lightly jogging to keep up with me.

"It could have been worse; everyone was perfectly civil. I felt like a right prat, though, when they brought up the GSA's budget."

"Don't worry about that; you said you were sorry and offered to pay for new flags. As far as they're concerned, you got yourself a clean slate. We've got better things to do than dwell on the past, especially with that Amnesty campaign coming up. I'm meeting up with Ben later to discuss the fundraiser."

"Ben?"

"Yes, Ben Weinberg, the guy who gave that speech earlier on about Abadi and Aziz."

"He seemed very well informed."

"Oh yes, he is, and he's considerate too. The other day, I had a flat tyre, and he helped me fix it after school. Didn't even have to ask."

"Sounds like a great guy."

Yousef turns slightly red.

"You're into him, Yousef?"

"Well, yeah, but he's quite popular. Don't think he would ever notice me in a romantic way."

"Why's that?"

"It's just that he's always dated these really popular girls. Although he says he's attracted to someone's personality, not their gender, I doubt I'm high up on his list of priorities."

"If you take him home to enjoy your mum's amazing cooking, he'll be on his knees by the end of the evening."

"Excuse me?"

"To propose, Yousef, oh my God, you really do like him, don't you?"

"My mum would turn into Bridezilla the minute I got engaged. Weddings are a big thing in our family."

"I'm sure they would love to have a guy like Ben as their son-in-law."

"Yeah, my parents are pretty cool about that. Not everyone in my family is, though. Some hold rather conservative views and find it hard to reconcile their religion with my sexuality."

"How on earth would *your* love life affect *their* faith?"

"They say that homosexuality is just not allowed. It's sinful and forbidden."

"Love based on respect and mutual consent is never a sin."

"My parents believe that God created diversity Himself, so we should not condemn each other or be ashamed of who we are."

"I'm glad your parents are so accepting of you, Yousef. I wish that on everyone."

Yousef is meeting Ben after school, so we say our goodbyes. I'm about to head outside; Mum's picking me up to go shopping. Don't know why, 'cause how many hoodies and checkered shirts does a teenage boy need? But it might be nice to spend some time together. There's never been a shortage of women involved in my life, despite growing up with two dads. But I've never had a mum to myself either. Although Kobe's mum seems a bit stressed and absent-minded at times, a shopping spree might just be what we both need. I check my phone to see if she's here yet.

Five missed calls from Mum. After the fifth call, she left a voicemail. I hardly recognise her high-pitched voice. Dad's become unwell during a meeting, and they're at the hospital. He's undergoing surgery.

I'm at the hospital trying to find my way to the ward my dad's in. I'm about to ask the receptionist in the lobby for directions when I spot my mum.

"Thank God you're here, Kobe."

"How's Dad?"

"He's in the intensive care unit, recovering from surgery."

"What happened?"

"He became unwell during a meeting with the city council. He had a heart attack. They found a blockage in a coronary artery, so they performed bypass surgery."

"Can we see him?"

"He's asleep. The doctor said that in an hour or so, we can visit him."

"Oh good, care for a cup of coffee while we wait?"

The hospital has a nice cafeteria with a rooftop terrace. The sun's out today, so we take our coffee and apple crumble and sit outside. If it weren't for Dad's heart surgery, this would have been quite nice, actually.

"How are you holding up, Mum?"

"It's been quite the day, Kobe. First, I had back-to-back meetings at the office about a deadline that was due last week, and then I got the call about your dad. If I hadn't been so preoccupied with work, I might have noticed something was off."

"There're a lot of things any of us could have done differently lately, Dad included. Might be best to look forward instead of back."

"I just don't know how we got here, Kobe; when you were

little, the three of us were so close. Tuesday Taco nights, making our own alcohol-free sangria. Then, on movie nights on Fridays, all of us curled up on the sofa in our PJs. Going to the zoo or the pool on weekends and playing board games on rainy days. Now, I can't even remember the last time we had a meal together."

"We could try doing some of those things again, Mum, although I'd probably try to spike the sangria this time."

Mum's laughing through her tears, which is a good thing. I finally get to see how she really feels. Then, a doctor signals our way. Dad woke up, and we can have five minutes with him. Mum goes in first to see how he's doing. I wait for her in the hallway. When she comes back, she looks relieved.

"The doctor says he will make a full recovery, although it will take some time before he's allowed back at the office. I'm going to take a sabbatical from work to look after him. You can go in and see your dad now, Kobe."

I go in quietly, not sure if he's still awake. Dad's hooked up to so many wires and cables, all ending up in machines that make bleeping sounds. I know it looks worse than it is, but I still hate to see him this helpless.

"Dad, are you awake?"

"Kobe, please come in and sit next to me on the bed, will you?"

"How are you feeling?"

"Not bad, though I've had better days. Looks like they're going to keep me here for a while."

"They'll take good care of you here, Dad, and when you get home, Mum and I will do the same."

"Oh, Kobe, you shouldn't have to take care of your old man."

"We're a family, remember? From now on, we'll all look

after each other."

"Wow, when did you get this mature?"

"It's about time I grew up. Now get some rest."

I quietly close the door behind me. All things considered, this could be the start of something new.

Kobe Dewinter

Lexi has saved me a spot at the back. I sit down next to her while Vikram and Robin take their usual seats. Practically, the whole town is here. This Kiki must be one heck of an important meeting. I look around and see Selma and Jess waving at me. Jaimy is sitting next to Selma, with his mum on his other side. To my surprise, I spot Josh at the front. When he turns around, I give him a brief nod. He has dark circles under his eyes, and his blond, tousled curls look like they could use some conditioner. Maybe the stress of co-directing the school's play has finally gotten to him, or there might be trouble in paradise. The Kiki is about to start when a man in purple robes walks up to the front and asks for everyone's attention.

"Good morning, and a warm welcome to all of you; I'm Geoff. I'd like to start with the announcements. The bridge in our park is undergoing renovation after an unfortunate incident concerning its railing. We're very happy to have Jai with us again and in good health."

Everyone is turning my way, so I give them a perfunctory smile.

"Stonewall High's annual play is less than a month away; don't forget to buy tickets. Josh Miller is here to tell us more about the upcoming event."

Josh gets up and addresses everyone present.

"Well, uhm, good morning. In three weeks' time, we hope to entertain you with this year's play. It's a modern interpretation of Jane Austen's *Sense and Sensibility*. We are working very hard to deliver an unforgettable performance to the best of our abilities. However, we could use a few more hands on makeup, catering and costumes. So please let me know if you can find some time to help us out."

Josh sits down, and Geoff takes the stage again.

"Before I forget, this week's bouquet goes to Mr and Mr Garcia. They've welcomed their first child into their home this week. A gorgeous baby boy called Nicolás. We wish them every happiness and hope he won't keep his daddies awake at night too much."

Everyone applauds, and the Garcias are beaming while holding their infant son up for everyone to see.

"Now that we've covered the announcements, it's time to reflect."

A passionate speech about the town's history, and on how Stonewall High got its name, follows. He talks about the people past and present who fought for LGBTQ+ rights, resulting in the peaceful and accepting community they built. According to Geoff, the future is never fixed. If we want to change the world for the better, we have to treasure the good things we've achieved and keep fighting against anything that makes people's lives miserable.

The speech is finished, and we all stand up. An elderly woman called Mrs Kent shuffles to the piano. Everyone is flipping through some sort of songbook. When Mrs Kent plays her first notes, the congregation joins in. It's a rendition of *True Colours*, a great song about not being afraid to be yourself. The meeting ends after the song. Everyone is pouring out into the great hall, where a lavish brunch buffet awaits us. I tell Lexi, Selma, and Jess that I will join them soon. I need a minute to myself. I wash my hands in the bathroom and look in the mirror. Jai's face is staring back at me.

It's one I've gotten used to over the past week. I feel moved by today's town meeting, also known as a Kiki. I've never been much of a church-going person. But this service feels different.

It's beautiful, unpretentious and pure. It celebrates love and diversity and encourages people to withhold any judgement over one another and to look after those in need. It doesn't impose rules from an ancient book but offers inspiring quotes from those who are fighting or fought for a better world. The service lasted just over half an hour, and everyone is digging into an amazing spread. I can't wait to attend next week, hopefully with Lexi by my side.

Jai Patel-Jones

I'm brewing a cup of peppermint tea using freshly plucked leaves from my tiny but flourishing herbal kitchen garden. I do not exactly have green fingers, but I have managed to grow and maintain a substantial amount of herbs. They are neatly lined up on the kitchen counter. So far, I have basil, dill, mint, oregano, parsley, rosemary, sage and thyme. Since my dad is on a strict diet that doesn't involve any caffeine, I've decided to introduce him to mint tea. I know I'm going to have to put up a fight to get him to drink it, so I add a chocolate chip cookie to sweeten the deal. Yesterday, Dad was released from the hospital. He made a great fuss over being wheeled to the parking lot in a chair pushed by a nurse. The doctor insisted, probably to protect the hospital from any slip-and-fall liability. Just as well because Dad is easily out of breath, and his eyes seem a bit unfocused now and then. We've made him a bed in his study downstairs, so he doesn't have to climb stairs. To make sure he doesn't do any work, we removed his laptop and briefcase. He secretly tried to join council meetings online using his iPhone. Mum found out and threatened to confiscate the only electronic device we left him with. We did install a TV and DVD player to entertain him; we're not monsters. So, he mainly spends his days watching Disney movies, rom-coms and documentaries, which I carefully selected. We don't want him to watch anything too exciting for fear it will set off his heart again. Mum is working from home. Her company was very understanding when she announced she had to shift her priorities. We have a nurse coming in once a day to check up on my dad; he takes his pulse and blood pressure, among other things. When I'm at school, I know Dad's being properly looked after. After school, I relieve Mum from her duties and take some of the work off her hands. It all sounds a bit half-hearted, like we're going through the motions just to keep him alive. That's not the case; we're all trying to be a family again more than ever.

It's just that Mum and Dad are quite set in their ways, and it's hard to break habits, even after all the medical upheaval. We're all struggling to find our place, but we're hell-bent on making this work.

When I told my dad I quit the soccer team, he took it far better than I expected. I briefly hesitated telling him at all, afraid of triggering his heart. But I want our relationship to be based on honesty, and sooner or later, he would have found out regardless.

He told me he wasn't such a big fan of Coach Bates anyway and that the team relied on me too much. He did try to get me to sign up for another team, but I told him I hadn't gotten around to looking into that. In due time, I will carefully drop that I'm not very much into ball games any more. I have other interests now, the GSA being one of them. This afternoon, we're doing a fundraiser at school for that Amnesty campaign about Abadi and Aziz, two men held in captivity because of their sexual orientation. We all have little stalls scattered around the entrance hall selling homemade products. Yousef and Ben are selling cupcakes and cookies. Kelly is doing nail art, and I made origami flowers. Since Valentine's Day is coming up, I hope it'll be a hit. Mr Blend is doing caricature drawings of students and teachers. Most teachers have promised to drop by for a portrait. So, after I serve Dad his cup of freshly brewed mint tea, I head off to school with origami flowers carefully wrapped in a duffel bag.

When I arrive at school, most stalls have been set up. Mine's next to Paquito's, which sells homemade tapas. It looks delicious, and I can't wait to fund the campaign by visiting his stall. But first, I have to sell some of my wares. I decorate my stall with fairy lights to give it that little something extra. I brought several vases from home to display my origami flowers. I made roses, daffodils, daisies, tulips, sunflowers and water lilies. I put a price list next to a vase of roses. There better be no haggling, 'cause it took me enough time and effort to pull this off. Luckily, Mum helped out a bit; it turns out she's got this hidden talent when it comes to origami lilies and daffodils. The bell announces the end of the last period, and students are starting to pour in. It's showtime.

After about an hour, I'm out of roses and sunflowers. I'm halfway through my stock of daisies and tulips, and someone insisted on buying a vase. My fellow fundraisers are doing quite well for themselves, too. The math department has a sweet tooth and bought most of the cupcakes and cookies. There is a long queue for Kelly's nail art services. Mr Blend is blotting his face with a paper towel. He's drawn fifteen caricatures so far. Paquito is flat out of tapas. I'm a bit disappointed I didn't get a chance to enjoy his treats, but I'm proud he's completely sold out.

"Hi, Kobe, your stall seems to be doing rather well."

Paquito has sauntered my way and is looking at my origami flowers.

"Oh, hi, Paquito, yeah, thank goodness Valentine's Day is coming up soon."

I turn slightly red; *Oh my God, why did I have to bring up Valentine?*

"Well, you're all out of roses, so there're going to be lots of romantic dates around here."

Now it's Paquito's turn to go red.

"Uhm, I guess so. You did pretty well, too, Paquito; you're all sold out."

"My dad made most of the tapas; he's really passionate about Hispanic cuisine."

"Lucky you, I would have loved to try some of it."

"You know what, why don't you come over sometime? I'll let you taste tapas way better than this."

Wait, what? Is Paquito inviting me over? To have tapas at his place? I'm at a loss for words.

"Uhm, that sounds great. I'd love to. Is there anything I can get *you*?"

"Well, I would love to bring one of those red roses home for my mum. It's her favourite flower. But I see you're all out of those."

"I can make you a new one from scratch. The art department has a storage closet. I'll just get some materials from there."

"If it's not too much trouble?"

"Not at all. Can you keep watch at my stall for a bit? I'll be back in a minute."

I take off at a trot, as I'm glad to be of service. The storage closet is in our art room. I flip on the lights and start looking for origami paper. It's a bit of a mess, but I finally spot some paper. It's a nice shade of pink instead of red, but that'll have to do for now. Then, the lights go off and it's pitch dark. Great, just my luck, a faulty light bulb. I hear footsteps; it's probably Mr Blend checking up on me. I'm about to call out to him when someone grabs my arms. Before I can make a sound, a hand is clammed shut over my mouth. I struggle to get my assailant off me, but I'm not strong enough. I notice a second person. I'm being dragged to the end of the storage closet by both of them.

I try kicking my way out, but they tie my legs together, and then my arms are tied behind my back. A wad of cloth is shoved down my throat. I gag, but I can't spit it out. I try to get up, but since my hands are literally tied, that's not an option. My assailants aren't finished yet, because I'm being doused in hair spray. Hang on, it smells different though; it's paint! I finally manage to spit out that disgusting piece of cloth, coughing my lungs out. Just as I'm about to scream my head off, my attackers call it a day. They shut the door and leave me behind in the dark.

Kobe Dewinter

School is about to get a whole lot more interesting. After an uneventful double period of math, a repetitive French class, and an IT class that lacked proper WiFi, I'm now in biology. It's sexual awareness week, so that means sex education is part of today's curriculum. Since we're seniors, most of us have seen it all. Let's see what they have in store for us. It can't be worse than the sex education class I had to sit through back home. My teacher tried to slap a condom on a banana, which didn't work since it was really crooked. So not only was said banana a poor representation of what the average penis looks like, but the condom tore, so the whole point of safe sex was rendered moot. After the crooked banana fiasco, we watched a video on how it's perfectly natural to touch yourself. This basically came down to watching a bunch of teenage actors fake masturbating on camera. At least, I hope it was fake.

Mrs Dewitt walks in with a flipchart sheet supported on a tripod. She makes sure everyone has a good view. We settle down in no time, and we're all ears. She grabs a marker pen and writes **CCSS** on the top sheet.

"These four letters are your basic code of conduct when it comes to intimacy within a relationship or just a random hook-up. Does anyone know what they stand for?"

There's some hushed whispering, but no one responds.

"All right then."

She turns back to her sheet and starts writing: Consent-

Communication-Safety-Sex.

"I'd like to walk you through each of those letters if you don't mind. As you can see, *'C'* stands for consent. Any activity that involves intimacy should always be with mutual consent. In other words, there's no me if we don't agree. That brings me to the next letter: communication. Talk to each other. Don't assume the other one knows how you feel, what you want, or what you like. Voice any concerns you have regarding anything that's on your mind. And please bear in mind that alcohol and drugs cloud your judgement and affect any form of communication between you, and your partner.

Then there's the *'S'*, which stands for safety. I cannot stress this enough: practice safe sex. Your health is the most important thing you have. Even though there are cures for most STDs these days, don't take any risks. Being safe is about self-respect and respecting the one you're with.

Any online tutorial can show you how to slip on a condom properly, but it's up to you to actually use one. So, always bring a Johnny and no barebacking! That brings me to our last letter, which is an *'S'* for sex. We all watch movies, series and shows on TV. Quite a lot of them involve people hooking up, making out and having sex. All of these scenes are choreographed to the last detail, and performed by professional actors with appealing bodies, assisted by intimacy coaches and make-up artists on the sidelines. That will not be the case when you are sleeping with someone. Keep your expectations realistic. Sex is not about having the same experience you saw in your favourite rom-com or movie. Figure it out together, and you'll get there or not and that's okay too."

We all just sit there and hang on to every word she says. This is not what I expected to hear and see today, but I'm glad I did. It's honest, to the point, and true. I've only ever been in one relationship with Dana. We were our firsts in everything, which felt both exciting and comfortable at the same time. We figured things out together and never took any risks. After Dana graduated, we quickly drifted apart. I was disappointed about it but not heartbroken. Our relationship had run its course.

There were no rebounds for me, I couldn't be bothered to hook up with anyone who didn't feel as special to me as Dana did. Until recently, that is. Lexi is amazing, but I don't know if she feels the same way. This is not my world, and I don't know for how long I'll be here.

Mrs DeWitt is on a roll because she started writing on a fresh sheet: Stealthing.

"Does anyone know what this means?"

No one reacts, so she continues.

"Stealthing is when you secretly take off your condom right before penetrating someone. I don't think I have to explain the health risks involved in stealthing, let alone the betrayal of trust. It's utterly reprehensible. Should you ever fall victim to such a heinous act, do not hesitate to report it. And that goes for many things regarding your body or sexuality. Whether it's physical or verbal harassment, bullying, revenge porn, or toxic behaviour on social media, please talk to someone. Some of you are eighteen or will be soon. Much of the stuff I just mentioned is punishable by law. So, think twice before you act on any of it. Most of you have a decent moral compass and wouldn't dream of doing anything like this; I know that. The thing is, people don't often talk about unacceptable behaviour, until it's too late. To sum up today's health class, enjoy your sexuality, whichever it is; enjoy dating and falling in love; enjoy sex; but always bear in mind the magic words: consent, safety, communication and let's add common decency as well. Mrs DeWitt starts gathering her stuff.

"A health class usually ends with the teacher handing out free condoms to encourage safe sex. I won't be doing that. Considering that a teacher's salary is nothing to brag about, you guys should be buying me those. Have a great day, everyone."

And she's gone, leaving us well-informed and a little overwhelmed.

Jai Patel-Jones

This is not how I expected my day to turn out. It started off great with the fundraiser, selling a bunch of origami flowers, and, best of all, Paquito inviting me over to his place. Then it went south really fast. As a result, I'm sitting in a storage closet, legs and arms tied by strips of fabric. That vile cloth pushed down my throat is lying next to me. After my attackers left, I screamed my head off, or at least I tried. I inhaled quite a bit of that spray paint, so my throat is sore and dry. All I can manage now is a pathetic croak or a pitiful whine. I sound like a gravely wounded animal about to be put out of its misery. I'm pondering what I did to deserve this or how on earth I could have brought this on myself. A revenge act from the GSA for being such a douche for years? I don't think so, we all get along really well now, and they even helped me decorate my stall. I have no nemesis to speak of unless... Of course, it has to be them; Jake and Roy. We don't speak any more, but when we come across each other in the hallways, they give me the stink eye.

I don't mind their silent treatment; I have nothing more to say to them. Yet I've always wondered if they would let me off the hook so easily. After all, I ruined their revenge act on Paquito in the bicycle shed the other day when I threatened to tell on them, and I didn't show up for our team's final soccer match. Come to think of it, as far as they're concerned, I'm a traitor. Great, I've figured out how I ended up here, but I still have no idea how to get out. Then I hear footsteps coming my way. That better not be Jake and Roy for another round of ass-kicking.

"Kobe, where are you? What's taking you so long?"

It's Paquito, I can't believe he came looking for me. I croak as loud as I can.

"Are you in here, Kobe?"

The door to the storage closet opens, and there he is. A sight for sore eyes, or in my case, a sore throat.

"Oh my God, Kobe, what happened?"

Paquito switches on the light. I squint at the sudden brightness. When my eyes have adjusted, I notice that they did not tie me up with random strips of fabric but with rainbow flags. The irony isn't lost on me.

"Thank God you're here, Paquito. I was beginning to worry I'd have to spend the night here."

Paquito kneels down at my side and starts untying me.

"I never wanted you to make a big fuss over one origami rose for me, so when you didn't come back, I came looking for you. This storage closet is so messy, I thought you might have tripped and gotten hurt."

"You're not that far off. I did get hurt, courtesy of Jake and Roy."

"What? Did they do this?"

"They're the only ones who have a score to settle with me."

"Oh God, Kobe, I'm so sorry your friends did this to you."

He wraps his arms around me in a tight embrace. I quite like it, so I let my head rest on his shoulder for a bit.

"They're not my friends, Paquito; they're a pair of sad alpha male wannabes with nothing going for them. Just like me a few weeks ago."

"Oh, but you've changed, Kobe. It takes guts to leave your friends, even though they were toxic."

"That's true; I'm all about making good choices now."

"Glad to hear it; how about we choose to get the heck out of here. Let's find a bathroom and get you cleaned up a bit."

Paquito hoists me up, and we leave.

"Uh, Kobe."

"Yes, Paquito?"

"Just realised I helped you get out of the closet."

And once again, the irony isn't lost on me.

Kobe Dewinter

Stonewall High's handball team is staring at me expectantly. I've signed up for try-outs, hoping that this will be more of my thing than step aerobics. I don't seem to have much competition 'cause I'm the only one who showed up today. The team's captain is called Lucas, a lanky boy with shoulder-length ginger hair. He looks at his clipboard as if expecting to see a substantial list of candidates. But it's just me. That doesn't seem to bother him at all. He looks me up and down before he starts.

"So, Jai, I'm a bit surprised to see you here today since you've never shown any interest in joining the team. It was more your boyfr… I mean Josh's cup of tea."

"I wanted to try something other than the class I was taking at the gym. I'm not bad with a ball, although I've never played this sport before."

"Let me take you through the main aspects of the game then. Each handball team has seven players: six out-court players and one goalkeeper. In addition, there are seven substitute players on the bench during a match. We currently have thirteen players. As you can see, we are a mixed-gender team, but make no mistake. We're all fierce and competitive. Marty over here is in a wheelchair. He can outmanoeuvre anyone in that chair *and* is damn fast too. He was last year's top scorer and is well on his way to pulling it off again this year."

I look over at Marty, who gives me a little wave. Wait, this must be *the* Marty Lexi told me about. Her brother's ex-boyfriend. Since Collin's with Lisa now, I doubt he'll be coming to see any more games.

"I could drone on explaining all the ins and outs, but it might be best if we just get started. We'll see if you pick things up along the way." Lucas continues.

So, we begin. Our practice session kicks off with a few warm-up exercises. Then there's a lot of throwing and catching balls and shooting on goal. In the last half hour, we play a match. It's more challenging than I thought it would be. If you're in possession of the ball, you're allowed to stand stationary for three seconds. Then, you may take three steps.

Any more is considered travelling, which will result in a turnover. This means that the other team gets to throw the ball in from whatever spot it is at that point. So, after your three steps, you either shoot, pass, or dribble the ball. I'm drenched in sweat when Lucas blows his whistle to signal the end of our practice session. He was right. Everyone is fierce, and no one holds back. That includes Marty, who is so agile that it's difficult to keep track of his moves. Before I hit the showers, Lucas walks up to me.

"So, Jai, what do you think?"

"I liked it a lot; everyone's so good at it."

"Don't worry, you weren't half bad yourself. You'll pick up the rest along the way."

"Does that mean you'll have me on the team?"

"As far as I'm concerned, it does; welcome to Team Stonewall High. I'll get you a pair of shorts and a jersey next practice."

I can't believe it worked out so well; I made the team. This Saturday, I'm having my first official game. Although I expect to be on the bench rather than out on the court, it's still nice to be part of the experience. I text Lexi to tell her the good news. She responds straight away with a heart eyes emoji, a tennis ball and a pair of lips.

Apart from the tennis ball, I quite like her emojis, so I send back some of my own. I carefully select the pictures. I want to come across as interested but not desperate or pushy. I click on a smiley face, a little goal and a cup of coffee. The last one being a subtle hint to a possible future date. I press send and notice a colossal mistake. My finger has apparently slipped on the last emoji, I accidentally sent her an eggplant. I could seriously sink through the floor right now. Before I can apologise and correct my mistake, she sends me a text back. It's an emoji of a peach paired with a winky face. Wow, it looks like Lexi's got game, too.

Jai Patel-Jones

It turns out karma's a bitch, 'cause Roy and Jake got suspended. I didn't grass on them, and neither did Paquito. But the cameras installed near the fire exit did give them away. After Jake and Roy left me in that storage closet, they decided to take the fastest route out, which happened to be the escape way down the hall. The school had a break-in last year. Trespassers entered through the emergency exit and went shopping in the IT lab. As a consequence, cameras were installed to prevent this from happening again. The janitor, Mr Fairview, saw footage of two students using an exit that is to remain closed unless there's an actual emergency. So, he notified Mr Calhoon. Initially, their unorthodox exit wasn't linked to assaulting me. But that's where Mr Blend comes in. He found the storage closet in utter chaos. Yellow spray paint everywhere, crumpled rainbow flags lying in a corner, and materials carelessly tossed aside. He reported his findings to Mr Calhoon since that storage closet is basically his man cave. Mr Calhoon noticed quite a few blotches of yellow paint on both Jake's and Roy's shoes. Well, you don't have to be Sherlock Holmes to connect the dots here. Parents were summoned to the school, and I received a lengthy apology under the watchful eye of Mr Calhoon.

In addition, they're suspended for a week, so all things considered all's well that ends well. And things will only get better. Tonight, I'm having tapas at Paquito's place.

After school, I go home to freshen up and change. I have the perfect outfit. Since my shopping trip with Mum was cancelled, I ordered a few things online. I bought a pair of green chinos combined with a blue and white striped shirt. I swapped my trainers for a pair of suede loafers. When I walk downstairs, Dad looks at me open-mouthed.

"Kobe, I've never seen you look so smart before. Not even when you dated Dana. Wait, are you going on a date? Who is the lucky girl?"

"Easy, Dad, I'm just having dinner at a friend's place. Paquito invited me over to have tapas with his family."

"Wait, Paquito? Isn't that the kid you and your friends used to joke about?"

"Yes, we did, and I very much regret that. We're friends now; he's pretty cool, actually."

Mum enters and takes a long look. Then she tears up a bit.

"Mum, are you okay?"

"I'm fine, love; it's just that I'm so proud of you. I love your outfit, but most of all, I love you. You seem so much more grown-up lately. You're kind, considerate, helpful and creative. Just like when you were younger. I'm glad to have that person back again."

"Thanks, Mum, but that person is about to be late; I really have to get going."

"Of course, darling, I bought some flowers for you to give to Mrs Hernandez; tell her I said hi."

Just as I'm about to leave, Mum leans in and whispers in my ear.

"You really do look handsome, dear; Paquito is one lucky boy."

I'm at the Hernandez residence. They live in a terraced house with a modest front yard. It's entirely paved, and bicycles are scattered all over. I recognise Paquito's bike among two others. There is a brass nameplate next to the doorbell. It says *Mr and Mrs Hernandez* along with their three children, listed underneath: *Paquito, Lucia and Elena*. I'm about to ring the doorbell when I see Paquito's face looming up behind the door.

"I thought it was you," he says, while letting me in.

"Hey, Paquito, nice house."

"Thanks. It's not big, but it's all we need."

We enter the living room. It's cosy and tastefully decorated. It has a tiled floor with floral patterns. The walls have earthy tones; one has a Mexican flag painted on it. The sofa and armchairs have brightly coloured prints. There is a huge wooden dining table with benches instead of chairs. An arched doorway leads to the kitchen. The smells emanating from it are delicious. On the sofa, there are two girls watching Frozen.

"Hi there," I say.

"This is my sister, Lucia; she's a junior at our school. You may have seen her around."

"Nice to meet you, Lucia."

Lucia looks like her older brother, but her features are a bit more delicate. She has the same dark brown eyes and thick, wavy hair as him. Even their long and luscious eyelashes look similar.

"This is Elena, my youngest sister; she goes to middle school."

Elena is the odd one out. Her hair is blonde and straight, and her eyes are a mixture of green and grey. She looks up and nods in acknowledgement. Then Paquito's parents join us.

"Hello, it's nice to meet you. I'm Mrs Hernandez, but please call me Anna. This is my husband, Luis."

"Pleasure to meet you, Mrs and Mr Hernandez; you have a

lovely home. My mum got you some flowers, and she says hi."

I keep rambling on for no particular reason. Luckily, Mrs Hernandez doesn't seem to notice.

"Wow, thank you, they're really nice. Luis, darling, can you put these in a vase, please? How are your parents, by the way? Must have been quite a scare having your dad in the hospital."

"Yes, it was, but he's doing much better. He's not allowed back at work yet, and he's on a strict diet, which he hates."

"I'll bet he does, but there's nothing wrong with a little diet now and then, is there, Luis?"

"I suppose not," says Mr Hernandez while patting his voluminous stomach. But not everyone has a wife who's such an excellent cook. You will find out soon enough, Kobe."

"Can't wait, Mr Hernandez; it smells delicious."

"I need another twenty minutes, boys," says Mrs Hernandez.

Mrs and Mr Hernandez retreat into the kitchen.

"Let's go upstairs; they'll call when dinner is ready." Paquito grabs my elbow and leads me up the stairs. I like the way he touches my arm, as if we've always been close and can't wait to be alone together. Or maybe that's just wishful thinking on my part. I'm pretty sure there's chemistry between us, but Paquito has so much history with the original Kobe. Don't know if we'll ever get past that. We enter his bedroom; it's small but neatly organised. Just like Yousef's. Only without the movie star posters. Over his desk are family pictures; some seem to be taken abroad.

"Those pictures are from last year's holiday in Mexico. We go every other year because it's quite expensive. We always stay at my abuelita's house."

Paquito points at a picture.

"She's my maternal grandmother; my abuelito passed away two years ago. She lives on a ranch. When she was widowed, my uncle moved in with his family. It's a beautiful place. Clean air, open space and breathtaking views. It's not a working ranch any more. They kept a goat or two, some chickens and a horse to keep her busy. Abuelita grew up with lots of livestock and all sorts of pets. She once kept a pet iguana she found dehydrated by the side of the road and nursed it back to health."

"Sounds like a wonderful place, Paquito. Wish I could see it for real."

"I'd love to take you there one day, Kobe."

With that, he slowly inches closer to me. He touches my arm, and I reach out to his. We stand there as if we're about to dance but forgot to put the music on. I close my eyes, not knowing what to do with myself. And then his lips are on mine. They feel smooth, velvety and warm all at once. I open my mouth a bit and kiss him back. His warm breath on my face feels comforting and safe. I lean in and kiss him again, more passionately this time.

His sighs trigger something inside of me that I kept locked up for so long. I basically threw away the key, come to think of it. Now that it's been set free, I can't hold back any longer. I wrap my arms around him while he shoves his hips hard against mine. Now, it's my turn to make inappropriate noises. When we finally resurface, I look up at him.

"That was awesome; when did you stop being mad at me, Paquito?"

"When you stood up for me in that bicycle shed."

"Took you long enough to let me know."

"You deserved your time in purgatory, but now you've earned your seven minutes in heaven."

"Seven minutes? That's all I'm getting? Well, I'm about to overstay my welcome."

Just as we start kissing again, Mrs Hernandez calls. Dinner is ready.

Kobe Dewinter

The three of us are all curled up on Jess's twin bed. According to Selma, a bestie date night was long overdue. We have popcorn and cheese puffs within arm's reach. *Bend it Like Beckham* is playing in the background; it's Jess's favourite movie. We're sipping Diet Coke with a little something extra called Jack Daniels. Never been much of a whiskey enthusiast, but combined with Coke it's not bad. It's not like we're binge-drinking. According to Selma, Jess is a lightweight. If she exceeds her alcohol limit, she falls into a deep sleep while keeping Selma awake with her snores. Selma claims she really needs her beauty sleep, so she keeps a sharp eye on Jess's J.D. and coke intake.

"Jai, how are things with Lexi?" Jess asks while cramming a handful of cheese puffs into her mouth.

"What do you mean, Jess?"

"Oh, come on, Jai," Selma chips in.

"You guys are flirting like there is no tomorrow. At our swim meet, at last Sunday's Kiki and at school. And didn't you tell me at lunch that the two of you are sexting?"

"Wait, what?" Jess jumps off her bed and stares at me accusingly.

"How come I didn't hear about that?"

"Cause you were in detention, Jess, for failing to do your math homework again, remember? And we weren't sexting. I accidentally sent her an eggplant emoji. She probably thought I was joking and sent me a peach back."

"Oh, Jai, for someone so smart, you can be really thick sometimes. I'm surprised the two of you haven't sucked face yet." Jess sighs.

"This Saturday, Jai has his first handball match; Lexi will be there for sure," Selma adds.

"In other words, if you win, you'll get a celebratory smooch, and if you lose, you'll get a sympathy kiss. Either way, you're in for a treat."

I'm not too sure about that. Flirting is one thing, but actually making a move? I haven't done anything noteworthy since Dana and I broke up. Not sure I know how to go about it any more.

"So, Selma, any news about the play your brother is co-directing?"

"I haven't seen much of Jaimy lately, to be honest. He spends most of his time in the auditorium, overseeing rehearsals. Any time he has left, he spends at Josh's place. As if those two aren't practically joined at the hip as co-directors. What could they possibly have left to talk about?"

"We spend most of our free time together, Selma. I think we still have lots to talk about."

"That's because you're the most interesting, beautiful and eloquent person I know, darling."

"Are you trying to flatter your way out of this?" Jess says, eyebrows raised.

"Wouldn't dare, pumpkin; I'd much rather kiss my way out of it."

Selma pulls Jess back onto the bed and gives her a lingering kiss on the lips.

"I think that's my cue to go, ladies," I say while getting up.

"Oh no, Jai, don't leave. We didn't mean to make you feel like a third wheel," Selma says guiltily.

"That's okay, I think I'm turning in early. Big game coming up. Although I doubt Lucas will give me any time on the court; I want to be well-rested just in case."

"That's very responsible of you, Jai; we should call it a night too, Jess. Any more J.D. and coke, and I'll be listening to your snores all night."

Jess responds by slamming a pillow in Selma's face, which is quickly returned by Selma doing the same. Only a few weeks ago, I would have loved to see a girl-on-girl pillow fight, let alone join one. I would have tried videoing it so I could brag about it to Jake and Roy afterwards. But that seems childish and immature now. This is not who I am any more, nor who I want to be.

This place has changed me for the better. Lexi, Vikram, Robin, Selma, Jess and my handball team all made me feel so welcome from the day I woke up here. They must have noticed how out of touch I was with everyday life, but they didn't call me out on it. They helped me, encouraged me, put their faith in me, and let me become someone I actually like. I hope I can prove my worth to them as a friend, a son, a teammate and maybe one day as a boyfriend.

Jai Patel-Jones

Mr and Mrs Hernandez put out an amazing spread. The dining table is covered in tapas. Cold and warm dishes are served in colourful ceramic bowls with matching spoons. There is so much to choose from, but I don't know where to start. Luckily, Paquito picks up on my bewilderment.

"Shall I put some of this on your plate, Kobe? I can tell you which dishes go well together, and when you've finished, *we* can go for *another round*."

I notice he puts a little too much emphasis on the 'we' and 'another round'. Looks like he's not just talking about the food. I've barely recovered from our previous session. When Mrs Hernandez called, I was in no position to come down because some part of me down south wasn't either. Fortunately, Paquito had the common sense to tell his mum we were about to finish up on a joint book report and needed another few minutes. It took us more than a few minutes. Let's just say I wasn't the only one sporting wood. So when we finally came down, the whole family was seated at the table, clearly waiting for us to join. Apart from Lucia's snide remark about whether our hard work has finally come to fruition, nobody makes any comment.

Soon enough, I am caught up in all the wonderful tastes, textures and smells of Mexican tapas. I can't stop telling Mr and Mrs Hernandez what brilliant chefs they are. They both beam at me while being praised for their skills and hard work. After dinner Mrs Hernandez insists I take some of the leftovers back to my parents. I have another hour left before I'm expected home. Paquito and I head back upstairs to his room.

"Paquito, I'm officially in love with your mum. She is so considerate, welcoming and an excellent cook."

"Oh, looks like I have a little competition, not to mention how my dad will feel about this. It just goes to show that a man's love is through his stomach."

"Lucky for you, it's not just my stomach."

I pull Paquito into a tight embrace and brush my lips against his. His mouth opens just enough to let his tongue caress mine. Soon enough, our situation south of the border is right back where it was before dinner. With Josh, I hadn't gone all the way yet, but feeling Paquito pressing against me, I have never felt so ready.

"Is it all right if I pick you up, Kobe?"

"Pick me up? I've got four inches on you. Are you sure?"

"Don't worry, I've got quite some upper body strength."

Surprisingly, he does. He lifts me up and carries me to his desk. The only thing that could have made this look any more like a rom-com movie scene would be if he had swept everything from his desk first. Instead, he sits me down and grabs my thighs. Then he slowly lifts my legs. Right now, we're groin to butt. Despite the desktop being unyielding to my backside, I wouldn't want to change positions for the world. When he presses against me, he moves slowly, making sure not to break eye contact.

"Is this all right, Kobe?"

"Hell yeah," is all I can manage.

The thin fabric of my chinos and the soft material of his sweatpants allows us to feel each other as if there are no barriers. I pull him in for a long and hard kiss. When we break apart, I feel like I'm about to lose it altogether. Paquito looks on the verge of something, too.

"Should we keep doing this? I'm about to go off like a fireworks display on the 4th of July."

"You're right; think of the mess we'll make."

I pull him in for one last kiss. There's a box of tissues on his desk. He yanks half of the contents from their container and shoves them down my pants. Then he lifts my upper legs and spreads them, leaving me in a knee-to-ear pose.

"I just took care of messy endings. Would you like to have a happy one now?"

This time, I can only nod. Paquito wastes no time, giving it his all. I start to moan uncontrollably, silently praying that the walls aren't thin. It doesn't take long before those fireworks go off, and boy, do they light up the sky. Paquito is sighing louder than I've ever heard. I sit up and pull him against me in a massive bear hug while grabbing his butt with both hands. That's enough to set him off, too. We collapse in each other's arms, both out of breath.

"Feels like I just ran the freakin' marathon," I manage to get out.

"There's nothing like a little dry hump cardio to stay in shape."

Thankfully, my chinos are stain-free and dry due to the wad of tissue paper down my pants. Paquito quickly changes into a clean pair of briefs and pyjama bottoms. I manage to steal a glance, and I'm as impressed as I thought I would be. Paquito saunters over and whispers in my ear.

"Like what you saw back there? As far as I'm concerned, it's all yours."

Kobe Dewinter

My first handball match is about to kick off. I'm on the bench with six other teammates. Lucas explained our game plan in the locker room.

The school we're playing against is last year's runner-up, so we've got our work cut out for us. Lucas has put six of his most experienced players out there. Of course, Marty is one of them. Right now, he's warming up by spinning his chair and popping a few wheelies. I'm not sure that's going to help, but it sure looks awesome. My friends and family are in the stands. I told them I was benched as one of the subs, but they insisted on coming anyway. I look up to see if I can spot them. Vikram, Robin and Lexi are huddled together while sipping soft drinks through a straw. Lexi sees me looking at them and waves enthusiastically. Robin and Vikram give me a thumbs up. Jess and Selma are a few seats down. Collin and Lisa have just joined them. When Jess spots me, she mouths, 'good luck'. After both teams have finished their warm-ups, we have a quick group meeting with the whole team. We go over our game plan one more time, and then Lucas gives us all a spirited pep talk.

"Let's do this, guys; we got this. Today is our day. We've never had a more experienced and skilled team. Don't let those runner-ups intimidate you. Let's show them who's boss this year. And for those who are benched, be ready to jump in at any time."

We all high-five each other, and then it's show time. We start off fairly strong by dominating the game. We're in possession of the ball more than the other team, and two shots on goal nearly go in. Then, the other team kicks it up a notch. They're not as fast as we are, but they throw the ball more accurately. Their first shot on goal goes in. Lucas is all riled up and yells instructions at everyone. We up our game too and score our first goal. Everyone in the stands goes wild. I swear I can hear Selma and Jess scream my name, even though I'm on the bench. Marty is as quick as ever and scores our second goal. At half-time, the other team leads by 13-11. Jason, one of our field players pulls a hamstring and is out. Lucas asks Karen to take his place. Wise choice, 'cause Karen is a fast and focused player. She proves her worth within minutes when she scores her first goal. About five minutes before the game ends, Marty is injured.

He hurt his arm trying to spin his chair and catch the ball at the same time. Lucas decides to bench Marty. We're currently tied 15-15, and the other team seems to be getting the upper hand. Lucas runs up to me.

"Patel-Jones, you're up!"

For a second, I wonder who that is before I realise it's me. I'm Patel-Jones; at least, that's who I am over here. I can't believe my luck. I actually get to play my first game. Hope I won't screw up and let everyone down. I join my team on the court, where the game's final minutes are about to start. I manage to keep up and pass the ball where it needs to go. Neither team attempts a shot on goal. It looks like it's going to be a tie. Then, the referee blows his whistle. Karen is reprimanded for travelling, which results in a turnover. Lucas objects vehemently, but to no avail. The opposing team is in possession of the ball with less than one minute to go. They leap at the chance of sealing the deal, and pass the ball around at high speed. One tall and burly player has a clear shot on goal. He throws the ball, but

I'm close by. I jump and smash the ball away from its target as hard as I can. The referee blows his whistle again, this time to signal the end of the game.

We're in the locker room, and Lucas is giving a speech.

"We didn't win today as we hoped. But all things considered, it wasn't a bad game. We stood our ground and gave it our all. Karen did a great job subbing for Jason, and then there's you, Jai."

"What about me?"

"You saved our asses by smashing that ball away from the goal in the last minute. If you hadn't done that, we would have lost. So, thank you, Jai. Well done."

I turn slightly red, but smile and nod in acknowledgement. After everyone has showered and changed, we head up to the upstairs cafeteria to have a drink. Jason's hamstring is doing a lot better; he's confident he'll be back in shape by our next game.

Marty's holding an ice pack in his injured hand. Although it's bruised, he can't wait to play again. Karen is a bit subdued. She feels bad about causing the other team to nearly make the winning point. Of course, it's not that simple. You win or lose as a team, not as an individual. By the time we leave the cafeteria, everyone's convinced we're going to knock it out of the park next time. We say our goodbyes, and I text Lexi. She offered to pick me up after the game. I'm looking forward to some alone time with her.

Jai Patel-Jones

I can't remember how I got home after my date with Paquito. As far as I'm concerned, I'm still walking on sunshine. This is all I ever wanted and more than I could have hoped for. After our very rocky start, I got to show him who I really am. He gave me another shot, and we hit it off like I never thought we would. Dad's already asleep when I come home, but Mum isn't.

"How was your evening, darling?"

"Great, Mum, Paquito's family is wonderful, and the food was delicious. Mrs Hernandez gave me some leftovers to take home with me."

"That is very generous of her. How are things with Paquito?"

"Never been better. Don't know what I did to deserve a second chance, but I am sure glad I got one."

"And I'm sure he is happy he gave you one, Kobe. Sometimes a new start and a different perspective is all you need."

She couldn't be more right.

"I'm off to bed, Mum. Goodnight."

"Goodnight, Kobe."

The minute I'm alone, I check my messages. One is from Yousef, asking how my date went. And if we're still on for tomorrow. Oh, shoot, I forgot. I'm meeting him and the rest of the GSA downtown to hand out flyers for the Amnesty campaign.

I text him back, telling him it went great, adding every food emoji I can find. He answers with a smiling face emoji, and wonders if I'm still able to walk around town after all that food. I send him back a thumbs up in reassurance. Then I scroll further down, Paquito has texted me.

Paquito: *Tonight was great for so many reasons. Can't wait till next time.*

Me: *Your family is amazing and the food was delicious. I liked dessert most of all.*

Paquito: *I'm still a bit peckish, though, wish I could put my mouth on something else.*

Me: *Anything particular in mind?*

Paquito texts me an egg plant emoji.

Me: *That's too bad, 'cause I make a mean sausage casserole. Can't wait to share that with someone.*

Paquito: *Someone?*

Me: *You silly, unless you want to stick to your vegan diet.*

Paquito: *Nope, bring on the meat. Just a warning, I'm a slow eater. I could take all night.*

Me: *As long as you chew your food carefully and swallow everything.*

Paquito: *Deal, promise I won't spill either.*

Me: *If you finish your plate like a good boy, I'm willing to bend over backwards to whip up dessert. Just let me know if you have any favourites.*

Paquito: *When?*

Me: *Tomorrow night, at my place.*

Paquito: *It's a date. Going to sleep now, so I can work up an appetite. Wouldn't want to disappoint you.*

Me: *Sweet dreams*

Holy Mikki! Our steamy text, or should I say, sext session, has left me wide awake. If this counts as foreplay, I can't imagine what the real deal will be like. I rummage through Kobe's drawers. There's lube and condoms. Great; whatever the night brings us, I'm prepared.

Kobe Dewinter

I am waiting for Lexi in the parking lot.

"Hey, Jai, great game. You really saved the day in that final minute."

"Thanks, but it's a team effort; anyone could have done that."

"But *you* did, and exactly at the right time. You should have seen your dads; they're so proud of you. They kept telling everyone, 'That's our boy'."

"Yep, they're all about team, Jai."

"And they're not the only ones; I've never heard Selma and Jess cheer that loud. Even Collin was on his feet, and I thought he wouldn't come because of Marty."

"So, the two of them have smoothed things out?"

"I wouldn't call it that. But he's happy with Lisa, and he isn't one to hold a grudge. Also, I told him you deserved all of our love and support."

"Wow, I'm flattered. But I was on the bench most of the game. It was a coincidence I got any playing time at all.

"I doubt it was. Lucas is hell-bent on winning and he will never take any risks. Especially not at such a crucial point in the match."

"Wow, looks like he sees something in me."

"Guess he's not the only one," Lexi says in a flirtatious tone.

I look at her and smile.

"Where do you want to hang out?"

"If you're still up for a walk, we can go to the city park. I brought a few snacks. We can have a picnic."

We walk to the park, talking about anything that comes to mind. Lexi is easy-going, and hanging out with her feels effortlessly. The park is peacefully quiet. Most families have left since it's close to sundown. I offer to carry her snack bag.

"Thank you, Jai. I suppose I have my hands free to hold on to something else now.

"To hold on to something else or someone else?" I tease.

"What do you think?"

Okay, she really wants me to make the first move.

"I think I'd like your newly available hand to hold mine, if you don't mind."

"Glad you asked, and I don't mind at all," Lexi says while slipping her hand into mine.

We come across a quaint wooden bridge. I've never been here before, but it feels familiar. Halfway down the bridge, shivers are running down my spine as I peer into the water below. Lexi notices my discomfort.

"Oh my God, Jai, I forgot. This is where the railing gave way. You took a tumble right here on this bridge. Are you all right?"

"Don't worry, Lexi, I'm fine; I just had a little flashback."

The flashback I had, felt like a distant memory. Only the memory wasn't mine; it was Jai's. When I peered into the water, I saw him. His face was tear-stained, and he looked very upset.

He was on this bridge when, all of a sudden, the railing gave way, and he tumbled down. The force of the impact knocked him out. Is this how Jai ended up in my world, and I'm in his? I remember seeing his face right before I passed out, but never realised what triggered him to trade places with me. We keep walking, and as soon as we've crossed the bridge, I feel better.

We stop at a wooden picnic bench and sit down.

"It's not much, but I brought some of those homemade scones and blueberry jam. And a bottle of diet coke to wash it down with."

"Sounds amazing, thanks, Lexi."

We dig in and enjoy the food and each other's company.

"So, Jai, what are your plans for next year after we graduate?"

Her question takes me by surprise, and I choke on my food.

"Whoa, easy there, no need to get all worked up."

"Sorry, it's just that I haven't given it much thought lately with all that's been going on."

"I understand; you used to say you wanted to go into fashion design."

I have no idea how to talk my way out of it. Back home, I couldn't wait to leave town and backpack my way through Australia. Guess that's not an option any more, but fashion design isn't either.

"I'm still undecided, I guess; what about you?"

"I want to go to law school."

"Law school? That's great. You're smart, a good listener and you are very convincing when you want to be."

"Thanks, any chance I can convince you to come sit on my side of the picnic bench?"

"Uhm, sure, why not." I change sides and sit down next to her.

"We're all out of food, anything else I can get you?"

"Maybe, but only if you're up for this."

I lean in a bit and so does Lexi. I brush my lips against hers. Then she kisses me back. A little hesitant at first, as if she's afraid

I might change my mind. But I don't. In fact, I lean in a bit more and wrap my arms around her. Lexi holds my face in her hands and kisses me again, with more confidence this time. When we break apart, we are both slightly out of breath.

"This is the best picnic I've ever been to."

"Probably because it's the only picnic where you got to kiss a girl?"

"Not just any girl; I got to kiss you."

"The sun is nearly down, Jai; we need to get going."

We walk back, holding hands the entire way. Crossing the bridge doesn't trigger any flashbacks or memories this time. We get into her car, and Lexi drops me off at my place. She opens the trunk, and I grab my sports bag.

"So, I guess this is goodbye for tonight," I say.

"Yep, I better head over to my place before my folks start wondering what's keeping me so long."

I put my bag down and take Lexi in my arms one more time. We kiss and it feels like coming home. Lexi ruffles my hair while simultaneously pulling me closer. I place my hands on her lower back and pull her into a tight hug. Lexi moans softly. I am hard in an instant. But hold on, so is she. I feel my erection press against hers. I pull away, confused.

"Uhm, Lexi, I'm not the only one with a boner. What's going on?"

"I'm trans, Jai; you've known that since middle school."

Wait, I know I haven't caught up with every detail of Jai's life, but I did not see this coming. I know I have to say something meaningful and reassuring, and I really want to. At the same time, I can't believe I'm making out with another dude.

"Lexi, I don't know what to say. I didn't know you were a dude."

"I'm not a dude, Jai. That's not how I feel or who I identify with. I'm Lexi, a girl in her senior year using she and her pronouns. Why are you so weird about this all of a sudden?"

"I just never thought of myself falling for a chick with a dick."

As soon as the words are out, I know they're bad. But I can't take them back or unsay what I just said. Lexi looks at me as if I slapped her in the face.

"Well, if that's what you think I am, then it's best if I leave," she says.

"Oh God, no, wait, Lexi, I'm so sorry. That's not what I meant. Wait, let me explain."

But Lexi drives off, wiping tears from her eyes as she looks at me in her rear-view mirror.

Jai Patel-Jones

Yousef is waiting for me in front of Burgers & You, a popular fast-food chain. He has a decent stack of flyers in his hands. At our last GSA meeting, we decided that a fundraiser wasn't enough to help queer communities overseas. Especially those living in oppressed and non-accepting regimes. We want to raise awareness of some of the challenges these people face on a daily basis. As a result, we're campaigning on the streets this morning. We want to cover as much ground as possible, so we've divided the city into sections. Everyone has paired up and works in a different part of town. We'll all meet up for lunch afterwards at Burgers & You. Paquito has paired up with Kelly, insisting on covering the lower east side. Coincidentally, it has Kelly's number-one nail salon and Paquito's favourite boutique. We let it slide because, why not seize the day when you can mix business with pleasure? Speaking of which, this morning, I quickly texted Paquito to see if we were still on for tonight. He texted me an eggplant/sausage emoji, so I'll take that as a yes.

Yousef and I hit the streets. Most people are willing to take a leaflet. I get it; why put your shopping spree on hold for a couple of teens telling gruesome stories about the violation of human rights? But there are some who understand what we're doing and give us a few minutes of their time. Around noon, we call it a day and head back to our agreed-upon lunch spot.

"Kobe, rumour has it your date with Paquito was muy

caliente," Yousef says, grinning from ear to ear.

"Jeez, Yousef, how long have you been holding back that joke?"

"Just thought of it, but seriously, dude, spill the beans."

"Well, we had tapas with his family, and then Paquito and I enjoyed a little dessert upstairs."

"Kobe, you dog. For real, I'm happy for you guys. It's just that…"

"It's just what Yousef?"

"Don't get me wrong, but not too long ago, you were as anti-gay as those oppressive regimes we're trying to tell people about. And didn't you used to date that senior called Dana? You guys were inseparable. So what I'm trying to figure out, what's your deal with Paquito? Are you trying to make up for douchey behaviour, or are you really into him? 'Cause I think he's really into you."

Oh, this is tricky. I can't explain to Yousef that I'm not Kobe, but Jai. A queer boy who was into Paquito the second he saw him. But Yousef isn't blind, and neither are all the others in the GSA.

"Look, Yousef, I've been soul-searching a lot lately. What I didn't want to admit to others and, most of all, to myself is that I'm bi. I've always secretly admired the GSA, and by being a total ass, I wouldn't have to own up to who I really am. Especially not to my friends and family."

"How are things with your parents now, Kobe?"

"A lot better, since my dad came back from the hospital. We're really trying to be a family again. That takes practice, though. I think my mum knows about us and is cool with that. Haven't told my dad yet; all in good time, I suppose."

"Glad to hear things are finally looking up for you, Kobe."

"Thanks, Yousef, but hey, what about you and Ben Weinberg? Any news on that front?"

"Not really. I've been wanting to ask him out on a date, but he never seems to be alone. He's always surrounded by a gang of handsome boys and pretty girls. Just looking at him makes me feel like a third wheel."

"Oh, Yousef, I'm so sorry to hear that. I'm sure if you could get him alone for a bit, he'd be all over you in no time."

"Well, I don't count on getting any alone time. Wherever he goes, he attracts a crowd. Look at this photo he just posted in our GSA group app."

I take a look and see Ben Weinberg surrounded by half of our crew. The photo is captioned: Look who I bumped into! God, he's right. It would be a herculean task to separate him from the herd. But you know what? Challenge accepted. I still feel that Yousef and Ben would go great together. They just need a bit of serendipity in their lives.

"Yousef, I truly believe you and Ben deserve a proper shot at love. I'll figure out how."

"You gonna play Cupid now, Kobe?"

"I go by many names, like Cupid, Eros and Amor. Once my arrow hits its target, there is no turning back from L-O-V-E."

Yousef is cracking up at my cheesy analogy. Good to see him smile again. Since my love life is working out so well, it's about time I help out my fellow queers.

Kobe Dewinter

How did this happen? My date with Lexi didn't just blow up; it went nuclear! And I'm to blame for that. I briefly consider going after her and beg her to hear me out. But that would just be another bad move. It's late, and no doubt Lexi is still very upset. When I walk into our living room, Vikram and Robin are watching their favourite TV show called *Ground-Breaking Gardening*.

"You see, Robin, I told you we should have planted daffodils instead of petunias?"

"Oh, Vikram, let's just wait and see what happens."

I clear my throat, just in case I'm interrupting a vital bit of ground-breaking gardening.

"Jai, darling, you're back. Your handball debut was amazing, love," Vikram says, beaming up at me.

"Definitely the man of the match, Jai. We're so proud of you," Robin jumps in.

I want to tell them it was a group effort, that my part in today's game was minimal, and everyone's contribution mattered. But I can't. I feel completely drained after what happened with Lexi. Robin and Vikram take a good look at me and see that something's off.

"Jai, are you all right, darling? You look a bit pale. Have you eaten?"

"Yes, darling, what's going on? I thought you were hanging out with Lexi after the game. Did you guys grab a bite to eat?"

At this point, I can't even talk any more. I sit down, tears streaming down my face. I'm in someone else's body. In a world that feels alien to me at best. I've managed to make friends, get involved in people's lives, join a sports team and, against all odds, find that special someone. Now I've ruined everything. I just don't know what to do any more.

"Things didn't go as planned with Lexi today?" Vikram asks carefully.

"That's an understatement," I practically howl.

"Easy, love, would you like to talk about it?" Robin wraps an arm around me.

"After the game, we went for a picnic in the park. Everything was fine, no wait, actually it was great. She really gets me, and I get her. After she dropped me off, well things got a bit, uhm, intimate." I stare at my feet, not able to look at either of my dads. But Vikram and Robin seem unperturbed.

"What happened next, darling?" Vikram asks.

"We kissed, which felt great. Then we hugged, and my lower half responded to that, but so did hers."

"But you've known Lexi for ages; why are you surprised?" Robin says.

"It's just that ever since I fell off that bridge, my memory glitches now and then. I don't remember that part about her. And worst of all, I made her feel like it was a big deal."

"Oh, sweetheart." Vikram sighs.

"Just give her some space, but let her know that when she's ready, you'd love to talk," Robin adds.

I go up to my room. I feel a little better after getting things off my chest with Vikram and Robin. They were so understanding, and they didn't even berate me for being so insensitive.

I feel like an ass nonetheless. But they're right. I need to give Lexi some space to heal, from me. I grab my phone and look at my messages.

Selma and Jess are dying to know how 'the afterparty' went. Lucas scheduled an extra training session in our group app for next week. Marty sent me a 'well done' and thumbs-up emoji about today's game. There's no text from Lexi. I want to take Robin's advice and let her know I'm here if she wants to talk. But every message I type seems utterly pointless. In the end, I just type emojis. I send her hearts in every colour of the rainbow flag.

I check my phone messages first thing in the morning. Nothing from Lexi. Maybe she'll come around when we see each other at school. We have maths together in the first period. I get dressed as quickly as I can. Robin has barely even started making breakfast when I grab a banana from the fruit bowl.

"I'm heading to school early this morning, got some homework to catch up with." I shout at him.

Giving Robin no time to second guess my swift exit and possibly comment on it, I leave. There is no sign of Lexi when I arrive at school. I am half an hour early; the only other kids at school are the ones who have early morning detention. Luckily, my locker is near the main entrance, so I can keep an eye on who comes in. My strategic stake-out doesn't make a difference; when the bell announces our first class, I haven't spotted Lexi anywhere. First period goes by in a haze. I have a free one next. Just as I'm about to check my messages for the umpteenth time, I spot Selma and Jess.

"Guys, good to see you. Have you seen Lexi today?"

"Good morning to you too, Jai," Selma says.

"Are you so smitten you can't go without her for one whole

period?" Jess says, while batting her eyelashes at me.

I realise I sound rather pathetic.

"No, it's just that Lexi and I aren't speaking."

"What? I thought you guys really hit it off," Selma says.

"We went on a date yesterday, and it was awesome. At the end of our date, I said something stupid, though, and now I don't know where we stand."

"Don't worry, Jai, Lexi has a big heart. I'm sure she'll forgive you if you apologise," Jess offers.

I wish it were that simple, but I don't want to share any further details of what happened last night. I walk to the library, hoping for some peace and quiet to think things over. I spot Collin browsing through a book about Tai Chi. I don't want to put him in the middle of this, since Lexi is his sister. Truth be told, I am kind of desperate.

"Hi, Collin, what are you reading?"

"Oh, hi, Jai, I'm reading this inspiring book about Tai Chi. Lisa and I are thinking about taking a class together. It's supposed to be even better for body and mind than yoga."

"Wow, Collin, that sounds great. Uhm, is Lexi at school today? I haven't seen her."

"Nope, she's at home, sick. Must have picked up that stomach bug that's been going around. I drink a glass of almond milk every morning, and I swear it does wonders for my digestive system."

"Right, well, uhm, tell her I said hi and wish her well from me."

"Will do, Jai."

Great, not only is Lexi not speaking to me, I make her physically sick. But I know just what to do to win her back. As soon as I am home, I get to work. The kitchen is usually Robin's domain, but today, it's mine. After I'm done, my workspace looks like an episode of MasterChef: chaotic, messy and sticky. But I'm happy with the results. I find a little wicker basket in our storage cupboard and put my home-baked treats in it. I cycle over to Lexi's place.

I want to ring the doorbell, but I have to respect her privacy and the space she needs right now. I put the basket on her doorstep and add a little note:

Dear Lexi,
I'm so sorry.
Please accept this peace offering.
Miss you, -x- Jai.
Then I leave.

Jai Patel-Jones

Our GSA group date at Burgers & you is a great success. Ben is telling us an anecdote about a guy on the streets he talked to about the campaign. When Ben told him Abadi and Aziz were imprisoned for their sexual orientation, he simply said 'good riddance' and wanted nothing to do with any of our so-called queer agenda.

"Of course, we respect everyone's opinion," adds Bryce, who paired up with Ben this morning.

"We most certainly do," Ben says, smiling mischievously.

"So, we told him 'goodbye', and let him get on with his day, didn't we, Ben?"

"Yep, but not before we left him a little parting gift. Which happened to be a jar of my multi-colour face glitter. It's not my fault I accidentally dropped it in his shopping bag; who knew the lid would come off so easily."

"So, this gentleman is having Coq au Queer tonight with a dash of rainbow-coloured sprinkles," Bryce finishes.

We all laugh at the image of Ben and Bryce giving that man a little payback. Most stories aren't as entertaining as the one we just heard, but it's nice to share experiences.

For all of us, it was our first time campaigning on the streets. While we wait for our burgers to arrive, Kelly shows off her perfectly styled acrylic nails.

"It was for a good cause, though," Kelly defends her detour.

"I gave a lengthy and passionate speech about LGBTQ+

rights to the entire nail salon."

"Oh, you mean to the old lady getting a pedicure. Didn't she fall asleep halfway through?" Paquito asks.

"You're one to judge, Paquito; what's in that shopping bag again?"

Paquito turns slightly red while holding onto a shopping bag with the logo of his favourite boutique.

"Oh, this. I happen to have an important function tonight for which I'd like to dress up. I've been told the chef is going to whip up a spectacular dessert," he says while casually looking my way.

Oh God, he's talking about tonight. He's going to dress up for me. Better bring my 'A' game.

After lunch, most of us go our separate ways. Ben and his loyal gang of fashionably styled disciples are going on a shopping spree. Kelly is heading home to vlog about her mani-pedi. Yousef's cousins are staying over this weekend; his mum texted him to come home straight after lunch. Paquito is going home to prep for our date, as he calls it. Luckily, my parents are away for the weekend. Dad's health is improving by the day. He realised he hadn't taken Mum out for a date in, well, ever. So, he booked a nice hotel and told her to be ready with an overnight bag around noon. Suits me just fine; it means we have the house to ourselves for as long as we want. Paquito told his parents we're watching a late-night movie at the cinema, so we've got at least until midnight.

He walks me over to my bike.

"Need any help preparing for dinner?"

"Nope, I'm good. Besides, I wouldn't want to share my recipe and its secret ingredients."

"Like eggplant and sausage?"

"And so much more, Paquito; just you wait and see. It will

blow your mind."

"Always in the mood to be blown."

Wow, for an introverted, slightly nerdy-looking guy, he leaves nothing to the imagination when with me. Strangely enough, that makes me feel honoured. Apparently, he feels safe enough around me to let his guard down and deliver questionable puns. I smile up at him.

"Well, let's see where the evening takes us."

Paquito takes a look around and gives me a quick peck on the lips. In my world, I wouldn't have hesitated to linger on his lips or brush my hands through his hair. Over here, I don't feel confident enough to do so in public. On the surface, people seem very open-minded and tolerant. But when directly confronted by queer love, some take offence or become very defensive. It still baffles me why love can't just be love for everyone.

Kobe Dewinter

I haven't heard from Lexi all week. She's back at school, though she avoids me whenever she can. When I sit at the back of the class, she chooses a seat in the front. During breaks, she hangs out with Collin, Lisa and their friends. When I walk by, Collin gives me a small wave, but Lexi pretends not to notice me. After school, she rushes home. Not that I would chase after her. Vikram advised me to respectfully keep my distance and by no means, ambush her. Robin agrees, claiming that if I force her into a conversation, she's not ready to have, I will make things worse. So I keep to myself or hang out with Selma and Jess. I go to handball practice and spend my evenings watching *Ground Breaking Gardening* with my dads. However, this Saturday I have plans. Selma, Jess and I are going to see the school's play, *a modern version of Sense & Sensibility*. Selma told me it would be okay if I didn't want to go, since my ex-boyfriend is co-directing it. Jai caught him making out with the other co-director, Jaimy. But I said I was fine. Josh never cheated on me, but on Jai. Besides, the only one I have feelings for and whom I sorely miss is Lexi. This play might just take my mind off things for a while.

    The auditorium is packed with students, teachers and parents. The curtains are closed, but there's an excited buzz going around. Then the lights go off, and Josh and Jaimy make their appearance on stage. Though clearly visible in the spotlights, I don't recognise them at first. They are both very smartly dressed in white waistcoats combined with a black tailcoat and pinstriped trousers. In their high-top hats, they look impeccably styled: elegant and debonair. I can see why Jai fell for Josh; he's a hunk.

"Highly esteemed ladies and gentlemen," Josh starts. "Welcome to tonight's performance of our contemporary interpretation of Jane Austen's Sense and Sensibility."

"Our cast of actors, singers and dancers have worked hard to bring you this show," Jaimy continues. "So, let's not dawdle any longer and let us travel all the way to rural England. To be precise, to Barton Cottage, Devonshire."

The curtains open, and behold, it's Barton Cottage. A distraught Mr Dashwood appears on stage, lamenting his bad fortune of having to move to a cottage in the countryside with his three adolescent bachelor sons, Elijah, Martin and Mark. Mr Dashwood is completely broke after his deceased wife left him with nothing. The family's fortunes went to an older sibling, so there he is, skint and desperate for his sons to marry into wealth. The plot pretty much follows the storyline of Austen's novel, though the play is set in modern-day England. The eldest son, Elijah, desperately checks his messages every few seconds to see if Mr Ferrars, whom he dotes on, has texted him back. When it turns out he hasn't, Elijah stalks him obsessively on social media. Martin, the second son, falls for an alluring exotic dancer called Ms Willow. They hit it off really well, but at the last moment, she dumps him for a dashing young man with a substantial inheritance. Martin is heartbroken and on a self-destructive path when the slightly older Colonel Brandon takes it upon himself to nurse poor Martin back to health.

Naturally, they all live happily ever after, so the play ends with Elijah marrying Mr Ferrars and Martin tying the knot with Colonel Brandon. When the curtains close, we all stand and applaud the amazing performances of everyone involved. Stonewall High's principal, Mrs Blake, gives a speech about the school's impressive track record of performing unforgettable plays every year. She praises Josh and Jaimy as excellent co-directors with promising futures in the performing arts industry. Although I am just a spectator, I'm proud to be part of tonight's performance.

After the last curtain call, we leave the auditorium. Selma and Jess are heading straight home; they have early morning swimming practice. I'm queuing in front of the cloakroom to get my coat. Three people down the queue, I spot Lexi. She's engrossed in her phone and doesn't look up.

I want to call out, but I have no idea what to say to her, especially since we're surrounded by so many people. I head outside to get my bike when I hear Lexi calling after me. She looks slightly paler than usual and catches her breath while jogging up to me.

"Jai, wait." Lexi huffs and puffs. "I thought it was you back there at the cloakroom."

"Uhm, yeah, it was. You wanted to see me?"

"Yes and no, I just don't know what to do with myself any more. I miss you, but I'm still so upset. I want to talk to you, but I'm afraid you won't tell me what I want or need to hear. What if you're not the guy I thought you were? What if it all ends here?"

That's when I decide to tell her who I really am.

"You're right, Lexi. I'm not the guy you thought I was. And I'm terrified to tell you why. Terrified of losing you and everyone else in this town."

"What are you talking about? What's going on?"

"Please bear with me; hear me out even when things don't make sense to you."

"Okay, I'm listening," Lexi says, looking less frustrated and more concerned by the second.

"I don't even know where to start; maybe I should just introduce myself."

"Why would you do that?"

"Because I'm not Jai. My name is Kobe Dewinter. I'm a senior at Milestone Academy. One day, I was cleaning bathrooms at my school, when I hit my head pretty badly. I woke up here as Jai, a guy who lives with his two dads called Vikram and Robin. I don't know why I'm here, how I got here or how to get back. I've been trying to figure out this place in the past few weeks 'cause it's a bit different than what I'm used to back home."

When I'm finished, Lexi stares at me open-mouthed. I'm starting to regret my decision to let her in on my body swap secret. Of course, she's not going to believe me. I must sound utterly insane. She'll probably tell Vikram and Robin, and they'll cart me off to the hospital in the blink of an eye.

"Jai, I mean, Kobe, I'm so sorry, I had no idea."

"Wait, you're not freaking out?"

"Oh, I totally am, but I believe you. I can smell bullshit from a mile away, and this is not it. To be honest, I did feel something was off with you for the past couple of weeks. I thought your memory loss was caused by the fall you made from that bridge. But the things you seemed to have forgotten were so weird and random. You couldn't find your locker at school. You didn't know what class you signed up for at the gym. Boy, you really suck at step aerobics, Kobe; Jai is at the top of his class. What about that book report you did on Romeo & Julius? Jai is a massive nerd who knows his classics. He knows that play by heart, and you were droning on about how weird it was that

Romeo didn't end up with his sister Juliet."

"I know I am incredibly out of my depth in this place. I've been so afraid people would notice."

"Oh, Kobe, you must have felt so lonely."

"At first, I was, but then I met Selma and Jess. I made friends at school, joined the handball team, dealt with Josh and Jaimy, and, best of all, I met you."

"Don't you miss your parents, Kobe, and your friends back home?"

"Things weren't great at home before I came here. Living with Vikram and Robin has been amazing. They're such dedicated and caring dads."

"Do they know about you?"

"I haven't told them. I am afraid they'll think I suffered a mental breakdown. And I don't want them to worry about Jai, their actual son, who isn't here."

"Where do you think he is?"

"I'm not sure, but I think he's living my life as Kobe, back in my world. Just before I passed out at school, I saw Jai's face staring up at me."

"Kobe, you keep talking about your home and this place as two different worlds. What makes you think that's true? It's not like you're from outer space, right?"

"Nope, although they do say that men are from Mars and women are from Venus. But seriously, some things are significantly different where I come from. I know I'm not as well-read as Jai, but the classics we read at school, the books I've come across in the library, and even tonight's play. They're all about queer romance. In my world, every great love story is as straight as an arrow."

"But why would anyone want to write love stories most

readers wouldn't be able to identify with?"

"Well, that's the thing, Lexi, where I'm from, most people are straight. Over here, your parents are the exception to the, let's say, queer rule. In my world, it's the other way around."

Jai Patel-Jones

Back home, I change into my favourite kitchen apron. It has a maroon-coloured print of frolicking sea mammals swimming wild and free. I bought a couple online the other day, since I do most of the cooking these days. Dad's diet calls for lots of veg and fish, and he needs to cut back on saturated fats. So no more take-outs if I can help it. Tonight, it's just me and Paquito. I've planned every course with care and precision. After all, I've got the Hernandez tapas extravaganza to live up to. The menu is loosely based on our steamy text session. For starters, I'm serving roasted eggplant rolls. The main course will be creamy sausage filled pasta, and for dessert, I'm baking lava cakes. In addition, I've been watching Martha Stewart's table setting tutorials online. Although I can fold a napkin into a swan, there's no way I can pull off all the lavish table decorations I've come across in her videos. So, in the end, I settle for a few strategically placed candles, a lace tablecloth and swan-folded napkins.

As I start cooking, I can't find the cream I need for my pasta. Since it's one of the key ingredients in my main course, I head out to buy some.

I leave the supermarket with the cream and a bottle of Chianti. I make an extra stop at the flower shop to buy a tablepiece. I choose one with roses, daisies, eucalyptus, pampas grass and dried palm. It turns out a bit bigger than I expected, so I can't hold it while cycling. I put the cream and Chianti in my backpack and place the tablepiece carefully on the luggage carrier of my bike. It's a lovely sunny day, and I'm in no hurry. I take a small detour and walk through the park. In front of me, there's a fifty-something couple holding hands. The two men are in deep conversation, but every so often, they stop for a kiss. Oh my God, they're so cute together. I can't help fantasising that's me and Paquito in the future. Romantic walks in the park are definitely on my to-do list now. The two men turn left, and I head the other way. I'm nearly home now; it's time to put the finishing touch on tonight's dinner preparations.

"Hey, stop that!" I turn around at the sudden noise and see a gang of five teens circling the couple who were just walking in front of me.

"What you gonna do about it, old fairy?" a bulky teen demands.

"Leave us alone and go home," one of the men answers.

"What if we don't, you fairies gonna cry about it?"

"No, but I will report you to the police," his partner says.

He takes out his phone, but before he can call for help, one of the teens snatches it from his hand. Both men are trying to take the phone back, but to no avail. The gang has started tossing it around as if playing a ballgame. One of the men catches the phone but is shoved aside by a lanky boy. He drops it, and its screen shatters to pieces.

"You are paying to get this fixed," he yells at them.

"Don't think so, old queen; take better care of your stuff next time."

I should have called the police or look for other people to come and help out. But the overwhelming rage I feel makes me decide otherwise. I park my bike, put my tablepiece down and walk up to the couple, still surrounded by teens.

"What the hell do you think you're doing? F**k off!" I

scream at them.

"Mind your own business," the lanky boy replies.

"This is my business now; get out of here."

"Or what, you gonna throw those roses and daisies at us?" Another one says, while pointing at my flower arrangement.

"Let's see if we can turn that piece of crap into a little bird's nest, Nancy-boy."

Oh no, they're about to destroy my tablepiece. What is wrong with people? One of the kids walks up to my bike. As I grab him by the shoulder, he turns around and lunges at me. I take a step back and trip over my tablepiece. I have nothing to hold on to as I fall backwards. Before my head hits the pavement, I remember I forgot to buy bittersweet chocolate for my lava cake.

Kobe Dewinter

Lexi is sitting cross-legged on her bed. I'm slumped in her desk chair, clutching a mug of scalding hot chocolate. We decided to move our conversation off the streets and into her home. It was getting dark and late, but we both felt there was still a lot of ground to cover between us. I texted Vikram, briefly explaining where I went after the play. He replied with a thumbs up and a blowing kiss emoji. Lexi's parents have gone to bed, and Collin is staying over at Lisa's house. He's having an early brunch at her grandparents'.

"I get why you're repulsed by my physique," Lexi whispers softly.

"Wait, what? No, I'm not. Why would you think that?"

"After our picnic at the park, I dropped you off at your place. We kissed, remember? You were completely freaked out."

"Oh God, Lexi, I know I was. But that had nothing to do with you. Jai has known you for years, but I've known you for weeks. I didn't know you were trans, and it caught me by surprise, especially after what happened in the park earlier. When we crossed that bridge, I had some sort of flashback that wasn't mine but Jai's. I saw him on the bridge, very upset. He stared into the water below, and then he fell. When we kissed back at my place, I realised how little I actually know about you. It reminded me of the fact that I'm an outsider, an imposter trying to lead someone else's life. And doing a terrible job of it, as it seems."

"You were caught off guard, Kobe. That's why I felt you

were being completely truthful when you called me a chick with a dick. That wasn't Jai talking; that was all you."

I'm about to cry.

"I am so sorry I called you that, Lexi. For a short moment, I did feel like my old self again. The immature, homophobic high school bully. That person I hate so much and hoped so hard to have left behind."

At this point, I'm actually crying, or sobbing more like it.

"I can't take back what I've said, Lexi, no matter how hard I wish. Please believe me when I say that you are beautiful, each and every part of you. I've been attracted to you from the moment we met. Remember when I emptied my locker of all the Josh memorabilia? When I told him off and said I had moved on? You were rooting for me, or actually slow-clapping. And that was awesome. You were standing there in your Grateful Dead shirt, unfazed by the scene I just caused. You were concerned for my well-being and told me you'd be there for me if I wanted to talk. I understand if you never want to see me again. Just wanted to say thanks for everything."

I get up, but as I'm about to leave the room, Lexi calls out to me.

"Kobe, wait."

Lexi gets up, too; her face looks as tear-stained as mine.

"I don't want you to leave. Who else is going to bake me those God-awful muffins you dumped on my doorstep."

I laugh through my tears.

"You got those?"

"Yep, and your little note too. I appreciated the gesture, but wasn't ready to talk to you yet. Collin enjoyed the heck out of your muffins, though. He ate most of them. Unfortunately, he spent the next day practically glued to the toilet. He's been drinking almond milk every day since. Says it does wonders for his stomach."

I laugh out loud now.

"So he told me at school. Did you know he's into Tai Chi?"

"Not surprised to hear that; leave it to Collin to come up with a hobby designed to keep senior citizens on their feet."

"So, Lexi, where does this leave us? Where do we stand?"

"If it were up to me, in your arms."

With that, she crosses the room and hugs me. I'm so happy, I cry again, feeling utterly ridiculous. Luckily, Lexi doesn't seem to mind. She looks up at me and kisses my tear-stained face.

Jai Patel-Jones

I wake up with a splitting headache. As I slowly open my eyes, I hear voices in the distance. My eyes need a minute to adjust to the fluorescent light that floods the room. There is a pungent smell of disinfectant and chlorine. The room I am in is soberly furnished. Next to my bed, there's a chair. There's a glass of water on the nightstand and a small cup containing two pills. I hoist myself up, instantly regretting the decision. Bolts of lightning are shooting through my peripheral vision, causing more pain. I take the pills from my nightstand and swallow them with small gulps of water. I close my eyes and go back to sleep.

When I wake up, I am feeling much better. The constant throbbing in my head is gone, and there are no more flashes of light obscuring my vision. I realise I'm in a hospital bed, but where? Last time I hit my head, ironically, in another city park, I ended up in Kobe's world. Does that mean I'm back in mine? I still look like Kobe, but what if I travelled back, body *and* soul this time? I'd be Jai, but with significant changes in skin colour and muscle tone. No doubt I would have some serious explaining to do. If I'm back home, I get to see my dads and hang out with Selma and Jess. But the thought of never seeing Paquito again leaves me heartbroken. And what about Yousef, Ben and the rest of the GSA? And then there's Kobe's parents, whom I grew fond of despite our rocky start. I didn't get to say goodbye to any of them. The door opens, and a nurse enters the room.

"How are you feeling?"

"Not bad, I suppose."

"I see you took those pain pills from your nightstand. Hope they made a difference."

"They sure did; how long have I been here?"

"You were taken to the hospital this afternoon; it's a little past eight now."

Oh no, my date with Paquito. He must have thought I stood him up. I feel tears welling up.

"There, there, nothing to worry about. You don't have a concussion, just a bruise and a big bump on your head. You are going to be fine," the nurse says, while patting my hand.

"Besides, you have visitors. Your mum and dad are here. Shall I let them in?"

Wait, my mum and dad. That means I'm still here. I heave a sigh of relief.

"Well, I'll take that as a yes; I'll go and get them."

Shortly after, my parents walk in.

"Darling, are you all right? We were so worried." Mum rushes over to my bedside and takes my hands in hers.

"Kobe, son, I can't believe what happened at the park. Don't worry; the police are on it. Believe me, they won't get away with this. And, uhm, how are you feeling?"

"I've been better, but not bad, all things considered. How did you know I was in the hospital? Thought you guys went away for the weekend."

"When they took you here, they searched your phone for emergency contact info. You still have that 1234 password, don't you? They called us, and we came straight away," Mum says.

"I'm so sorry I ruined your date night."

"Don't be daft, Kobe; you didn't ruin anything. We're just

glad you're going to be okay. They want to keep you here overnight for observation. You should be back home by tomorrow morning, though. We'll be here to pick you up," Dad says.

"Speaking of date night, there is a special someone who dropped by if you're still up for another visit," Mum says, smiling broadly.

"Who are you talking about?"

"Paquito, of course, we knew you were seeing him tonight. We phoned him and explained what happened. Although it's well past visiting hours, the nurse says she'll be lenient just this once."

Mum gets up and kisses me on the cheek. Dad pats me on the shoulder, and they leave.

I can't believe he's here. I must be dreaming. But I'm not, because there he is, holding an absurdly large bouquet of flowers.

Kobe Dewinter

We are both sitting cross-legged on Lexi's bed. We lost ourselves in hugs and kisses for a while, which felt great. I would have gladly settled for friendship or even just a 'hi' in the hallways at school. But when we kissed, it felt like we picked up right where we left off.

"I'd really like to get to know you properly. I don't share any of Jai's memories about all those past years."

"That's not on you, Kobe. I can't imagine what it must have been like, waking up in a strange house with someone else's parents and friends. I would have lost my mind if it were me."

"You really helped me fill in the blanks of Jai's life."

"So, what do you want to know about me?"

"If you don't mind telling me, what was it like growing up trans?"

"I was born as Alexander, but from early on, people just called me Lexi. As a kid, I never really identified with my gender given at birth. No one in my family or anyone else in this town batted an eyelid. I wore dresses, played with dolls and got on with my life just like any other girl. I never felt excluded or that I didn't belong."

"Wow, that sounds great. In my world social acceptance isn't that easy. I've heard stories about trans people's struggles. Where I'm from, some people are seriously bothered by trans women using certain public facilities, suggesting they make cisgender women feel uncomfortable or unsafe when using the ladies."

"But that's awful, discriminatory and humiliating."

"I know. My dad back home is the deputy mayor of my town. He told me about council meetings where trans rights were discussed. Emotions would always run high with both supporters and opponents. Some people feel that being trans is an alternative lifestyle you purposefully choose over being mainstream or cisgender. Social acceptance might become easier when you have the right identification documents. Getting those documents can be a lengthy and complicated process."

"I can't believe that complete strangers get to have an opinion on your identity and have the legal power to exclude you under the false pretext of feeling unsafe. When I was twelve, I got my first ID card. I filled in female as my gender and told them I was trans. That was it."

"I'm glad your transition on paper went smoothly."

"I started taking puberty blockers when I went to high school. When I turn eighteen, I'll have my top surgery. I'm using breast prostheses in the meantime. I'm not so sure about having bottom surgery, though. Right now, it doesn't feel like an essential part of my transition process. My doctor says that gender affirmation is a different journey for everyone."

"Wherever your journey takes you, I'll be there for you."

"Thanks, Kobe; I do have my so-called dysphoria days. That's when I feel frustrated and stressed out about my gender not matching my body."

I crawl over to her and take her in my arms. All I want is to make her happy and protect her from any evil, even though we live in this easy-going, beautiful queer world. Lexi cradles my face and gently places kisses on every feature. Then she works her way down and starts kissing my neck. It feels so insanely good that I temporarily lose the ability to speak. When she asks if she can take my shirt off, I nod and let her silky-smooth hands caress me. I ask if it's all right to take off hers. She takes my hands and guides them. When we're both topless, I lie down and take her in my arms. Every part of her feels warm and soft to my touch. I completely lose track of time, drowning in her kisses and tender embrace. When I hear an incoming text message, it's well past midnight.

"Lexi, I should be going; Vikram just texted me."

"I'd love for you to stay over."

"Are your parents okay with that?"

"Oh, please, Lisa practically lives here on weekends."

So, I text Vikram and tell him I'll be back the next morning. Lexi and I crawl under the covers and fall asleep in each other's arms.

Jai Patel-Jones

Paquito looks as if he's about to drop his flowers when he sees me. As he walks towards my bed, I notice how pale he looks. His hair is sticking up every which way, and his lower lip is quivering. I'm starting to feel worried; he looks worse than me.

"Are you all right?" I ask carefully.

Paquito throws his flowers on my nightstand and bursts into tears.

"Oh my God, Kobe, I can't believe what happened. You're in the hospital."

I take Paquito's hand and pull him next to me.

"Don't worry. I'm fine. The nurse says it's just a bruise and a bump. I get to go home in the morning."

"Sorry for bawling my eyes out; you're the one who got attacked. I'm making this all about me."

"It's okay, I understand. This is not the meet-cute I had in mind for tonight. But I'm so happy you're here, Paquito; it's been awful."

Paquito wraps his arms around me and hugs me carefully.

"Do you want to talk about it, Kobe?"

"There's not much to tell; I saw two men being hate-crimed by a group of kids. I lost it and stepped in; as you can see, that didn't end well."

"That was very brave of you, Kobe."

"Stupid, more like it. I should have called the police or looked for help. Anything would have been better than what I did."

"Well, it wasn't the safest way to interfere like that, but probably the fastest way to help. Who knows what would have happened to those men if you hadn't stopped them."

"You know what bothers me most about all of this? I was walking a few steps behind them on my way home. They were holding hands, and all I could think of was that's what I want when I'm their age. Going on walks with the person you love, holding hands and reminiscing about your life together. Like dates you've been on, anniversaries, holidays, and maybe even the breakups and makeups. 'Cause sharing your life with someone is not just about the good days, but about the bad and the ugly ones, too. In my mind, they were the perfect picture until those bullies swooped in and ruined everything. It's not just a stroll in the park they wrecked, but something way worse. They destroyed their sense of security and their right to hold hands in public without putting themselves, or the person they love at risk. Those men will never venture out carefree again, always thinking twice about showing affection in public."

"I know it's not right, Kobe, but sadly, not everyone is accepting of queer love. That's why GSAs are so important, and campaigning on the streets, and celebrating Pride. Let's show everyone that love trumps hate, prejudice and bigotry. Let's show them queer cuddles and kisses are as wonderful as straight ones."

"Speaking of which, can you show me just how wonderful?" I ask Paquito, casually.

He slides over a little closer on the bed and carefully lifts my chin so we're face-to-face.

"Just tell me if it hurts."

His kisses are cautious and slow, as if I'm made of glass and will break at the slightest touch. I run my hands through his hair, gently pulling him closer to me. Our hugs and kisses become more intense. Paquito supports the back of my neck so he can nuzzle my throat. His lips and nose brushing against every inch of my skin, make me forget where I am. Till his fingers accidentally nudge the bump at the back of my head.

"Ouch!" I yell.

"Oh, shoot," Paquito says. "Are you all right, Kobe? I'm so sorry. I got carried away. You must be bruised all over."

"I'm fine; it's actually just my head. It felt so good, I forgot about that bump."

"Maybe it's safer if we move things a little more down south?"

"I'm listening."

"Lie down, Kobe. Put your head on that pillow. Are you comfortable?"

I am suddenly very much aware of the hospital gown I'm wearing.

"Oh God, look at what they put me in; I look absurd, Paquito."

"Well, it's not as if you had time to pack a suitcase full of fancy nightwear before they brought you in. But you know what? This gown suits me just fine for what I'm about to do."

And he's right. He very gently flips me on my side. Then, he unties my hospital gown at the back by pulling at the strings. They come undone easily. He slides down a bit, placing a hand on my hip. Then his lips are on my shoulders. He slowly works his way down, following the curve of my spine. When he's at the small of my back, he starts massaging my hips while kissing those little dimples just above my backside. At this point, I'm so full of natural endorphins that I could make a headstand if I wanted to. I turn around so I can look at him. I wrap my arms around him and explore every inch of his face with my lips. His warm hands are all over my butt, stroking, patting and kneading. I am writhing in his arms while desperately trying not to let my mouth break contact with his. When we do break apart, gasping for air, I'm on the verge of soiling an actual hospital bed.

"I think we should stop; what if the nurse walks in? I can't stain these sheets, God; that would be embarrassing," I ramble on.

"Easy there; if you want us to stop, that's okay, Kobe. But you know that I'm a master of happy endings, not messy ones, remember?"

I nod, and he walks to the ensuite bathroom. He comes back with a towel. He shoves it underneath my gown, covering the bits that would definitely make a mess.

"So, what do you think?" he asks.

I answer by cupping his face and kissing the tip of his adorable button-shaped nose. He takes me in his arms and pulls me on top of him.

"Wouldn't want you to bang your head, not even on a pillow," is the last thing he tells me.

Then his hands are all over me again. Touching, rubbing and fondling every part of my back. I kiss, nibble, and lick my way down his throat. When I gently nip him behind his ear he goes perfectly still. Just as I think he's not into that sort of thing, he starts to tremble uncontrollably underneath me. Guess I hit the right spot after all. He grabs my hips and starts grinding his against mine. Doesn't take me long to soil that towel. Afterwards, we lie panting in each other's arms. We hear the nurse doing her final round before her shift ends. Paquito dumps the towel in a laundry basket in the corner of the room.

The state of his clothes is acceptable, mainly because he's

wearing an oversized hoodie covering the sticky bits. He finds a vase underneath the sink for the flowers we carelessly left on my nightstand. Before he leaves, he whispers in my ear.

"Too bad we missed out on dinner, but that was one hell of a dessert."

I couldn't agree with him more.

Kobe Dewinter

It's been a couple of weeks since I've patched things up with Lexi. We have both updated our relationship status on social media, so everyone knows we're together. We hold hands at school, steal kisses between classes and, best of all, Lexi lets me nick her French fries for lunch. She calls me Jai when we're in public. Lexi's still the only one who knows who I really am. Seeing how complicated things could get if I shared my secret with the rest of the town, we agreed it's best to keep it on the down-low. Now that we're a couple, everyone wants to share in our happiness by going on double dates. Vikram and Robin uncorked a bottle of Prosecco when we told them we were dating. Ever since, they've been trying to get us to watch *Ground Breaking Gardening* with them. Luckily, we've been able to come up with excuses so far. Collin and Lisa said they thought we'd been a couple for months, and they wondered when we would finally go public. Lisa signed us up for couples Tai Chi. We didn't want to hurt her feelings, so we went to one class with them. During the *White Crane Spreads its Wings* exercise, we both feigned an injury, which, surprisingly, they believed.

Collin has been handing me small bottles of almond milk at lunch since we bailed out on Tai Chi. Supposedly, it helps me tone up my muscles and improve my posture. It tastes like feet, though. But as far as I'm concerned, it's a small price to pay for dodging senior citizens' PE.

Right now, we're having lunch with Selma and Jess to discuss tomorrow's school dance.

"It's a date, right? The four of us are going together," Jess asks for the tenth time.

"Of course, Jess. Any idea on what you're going to wear?" Lexi asks, while chucking her bottle of almond milk in the bin.

"Yes, we have," Selma says. "I love this year's theme. The roaring twenties: live now, pay later. We went on a shopping spree last weekend. Couldn't find anything close to what we were looking for. Until we stumbled upon that little vintage shop. They had this amazing black-and-white Charleston dress with matching gloves and a feathered headband. Can't wait to show it off."

"What did you get, Jess?" I ask her.

"I'm not really one for dresses, but I got this gorgeous three-piece suit. Shirt, sleeveless vest, Panama hat, suspenders, tie, the whole works. Oh, and there's this silver-coloured pocket watch."

"Wow, that sounds amazing, Jess; Lexi won't tell me what she's wearing, will you, darling?"

"Nope, sweetheart, it's a surprise. All you need to know is to pick me up at seven."

"So, no matching outfits for you two lovebirds?" Selma asks.

"Vikram and Robin told me they'd take care of my costume. I'm not into shopping, so I'm glad they're helping me out."

Leave it up to Vikram and Robin to come up with an eye-catcher. They got me a navy-blue three-piece tailcoat tuxedo, including a top hat, a white kerchief for my breast pocket, and a walking cane. Not sure if my outfit has that twenties vibe, though. I look like a Charles Dickens character, to be precise, a younger version of Scrooge. My dads think I'm the personification of a dashing twenties gentleman. They can't stop taking pictures, until I threaten to take the whole thing off.

It's Saturday night, and I'm driving over to Lexi's to pick her up. Lisa and Collin will hitch a ride with us. We're meeting Selma and Jess at the school entrance. As I pull up on Lexi's driveway, I have this ominous feeling that I won't be here for much longer. It's this gut-wrenching sense I had before when that mirror was about to hit me. I don't know what to make of it. Still haven't figured out how to get back to my world, but I'm not so sure I want to any more. Lexi has become very important to me.

It might be a bit soon for the *'L'* word, but I can't imagine my life without her. I can't afford to freak out right before my first big social function with an actual date, so I put my feelings aside for now.

Collin and Lisa are waiting in the doorway as I walk up to the house. They're both wearing sky-blue matching yoga outfits.

"I thought you guys were coming to the dance with us tonight. You didn't want to cancel your yoga class?"

"We are coming to the dance, Jai. This is what we're wearing. Yoga was introduced in the twenties over here. This is what yoga instructors wore back then. I think we really nailed it."

I'm speechless. Lisa is wearing a crop top over harem pants, and Collin's wearing tight leggings and a tie-dye shirt. Luckily, Lexi shows up. She looks astonishing. She's wearing a green twenties cocktail dress with embroidered sequins. She has long black gloves on her slender and elegant arms. There's a silver hairpin with tiny black feathers in her hair. Long strings of ivory pearl beads top off her gorgeous outfit.

"Lexi, you look beautiful. I don't know what to say."

"Thanks, Jai. You look pretty dashing."

"That's what Robin and Vikram said, I'm glad you agree."

Lexi's parents pop up with a camera, ushering us all into the living room for a group photo. I'll bet no one in their right mind would be able to tell what sort of party we dressed up for. My closest guess would be a cocktail party in a twenties Ashram with a Dickens theme.

I take Lexi's arm, as we walk up to the car. I open the door for her like a truly refined twenties man. However this night will turn out, I'm happy to have her by my side.

Jai Patel-Jones

Kelly is painting little rainbow flags on my forehead and cheeks. She feels nail art and face painting aren't that different. Meanwhile, Bryce and Ben are putting the finishing touch on their custom-made T-shirts. Bryce's says 'Born to be Gay' with lots of added glitter.

Ben's says 'More Pan than Peter' with a pink, yellow and blue flag painted at the top. Paquito is hunched over a map of the city centre. In a bit, we'll be walking there with thousands of other people, celebrating our identities and protesting violations of LGBTQ+ rights anywhere. There are no Pride parades where I'm from. My world is queer, to begin with. Being straight is the exception, not the rule. Moreover, gender-related rights will never be a point of debate since love, acceptance and inclusion are the core values of our society. We share and celebrate those values at our Sunday morning town meetings, also known as Kiki. This world could seriously do with one. I could throw one myself; nothing beats a good old Kiki followed by a lavish brunch. The problem is, I'm not sure how much longer I get to be here. I've had this strange sensation in the pit of my stomach all day. Like I'm about to have some sort of out-of-body experience. I don't want to think about that now, 'cause wherever this day will take me, I have one more job to do.

I walk up to Ben's locker and stick a note on it. I have folded this tiny origami rose, which I tape next to it. Then I walk over to Yousef's locker and do the same. I have no idea how this will play out, but I promised Yousef a little help from Cupid, aka me. It's nearly time to go now. Mr Blend is handing out rainbow flags. In our GSA meetings, we made several signs for Pride. Ben's sign says, *'One of my best friends is straight'* Mr Blend painted a *'Love wins'* poster in all the colours of the rainbow.

Yousef spray painted a sign that says, *'The only choice I ever made was to be myself,'* and my favourite of all is from Kelly: *'Harry Potter taught us no one deserves to live in a closet.'*

"Okay, guys, remember what we talked about? We stick together as a group. Don't forget to hydrate, and most importantly, be proud and say it out loud!"

We all cheer 'cause proud is what we are. I walk over to Paquito, who is still studying the map.

"Hey, afraid we'll get lost out there?"

"Hi, I just want to make sure the parade route won't take us through the park."

"That's really sweet of you, but I'm fine, Paquito. Don't worry."

It's been several weeks since the attack. As the nurse predicted, I made a swift and full recovery. Although I am seriously rattled by the incident, I feel safe walking the streets. I know there's more good out there than bad. Besides, I won't let a couple of bullies sabotage my sense of security, or well-being when I go out. My family seems to think otherwise, though. My dad's been filing one proposition after another with the city council to get more security measures in parks and on the streets. Of course, that's not magically going to solve hate crime-related problems, but he means well.

Mum's been driving me around town as if I were an A-list celebrity, constantly reminding me it's better to be safe than sorry. And then there's Paquito, who worries about me most of all. The first week after the attack, he insisted on escorting me home after school, though he lives on the other side of town. He wants to stay in on date nights or weekends, supposedly so we can enjoy more privacy. The truth is, he doesn't want to risk a repeat of what happened to me in the park. So, there've been lots of family dinners, game nights with my parents and watching Disney movies with Paquito's sisters. The only upside of staying in, is getting some alone time in either his, or my bedroom. We've been taking things slow, though. It took some time before my head was completely pain-free, not leaving much room for wild adventures in the sack. Also, I've been having trouble getting out of my own head when I'm alone with Paquito. I want to tell him who I really am, but I have no idea where to even start.

Every date we've been on, and every hug and kiss we have shared are all based on a relationship that isn't real. He thinks he's dating Kobe, a reformed bully who coincidentally turned out to be bi. Paquito has been very patient and understanding, assuming I'm still processing my attack. I'm going to tell him after the parade; it's now or never.

The streets are packed with people waving flags in all sorts of colours. The march starts at noon, and we're all set and ready to go. Music is blasting from speakers as we begin walking the parade's route. I'm holding hands with Paquito while taking in the spectacle around me. It's quite overwhelming, to be honest. I feel honoured to be walking among this beautiful group of queer people, celebrating their identities, while at the same time protesting prejudice, bigotry and hate against our colourful community. Along the route, we're being cheered on by spectators, most of them adorned with rainbow-coloured accessories. Halfway through our march, we stumble upon a different crowd. There's a group of people holding up signs.

Their posters are of a totally different nature than ours. I squint my eyes so I can read them. One sign says, *'If Adam were gay, you wouldn't be here today.'* Another one claims, *'It's Adam & Eve, not Adam & Steve,'* and an elderly couple is holding up a sign saying, *'I support biblical marriage.'* Wow, this is new to me and, frankly, quite shocking. But I've come up with an idea. I have a felt tip in my pocket, and there's a piece of discarded cardboard lying around. I start writing on it, and when I'm finished, I walk up to the elderly couple, showing them my sign: *'Don't use your faith to spread ignorance and hate.'* Everyone around me is cheering and clapping. And then Katrina and the Waves *Love Shine a Light* is blasting through the speakers. This feels like it is meant to be; they're playing my favourite song. One I have sung at so many Kikis throughout the years. We all start singing and dancing. Ben and Yousef walk up to the frontline, jumping up and down, waving their flags at the anti-gay brigade and their homophobic signs. Then it's time to move on. Ben sends a couple of hand-blown kisses their way as a final goodbye, and then takes Yousef by the hand.

Kobe Dewinter

As we pull up in the school's parking lot, I see Selma and Jess, who've just parked their cars. They walk up to us as we get out.

"Oh my God, Jai, you look amazing. And Lexi, you gorgeous girl," Jess says, while beaming at us.

"You ladies look great too; love your suit, Jess," Lexi replies.

"Uhm, Collin, did Jai pick you guys up straight after yoga class?"

"Nope," I quickly say. "Yoga was introduced over here in the twenties; they're yoga instructors."

Before anyone can say anything else about their unconventional outfits, we head towards the school's entrance. I have to give it to Stonewall High; they pulled out all the stops for this roaring twenties theme. At the entrance, there is a gold, silver and black-coloured balloon arch. There's a Great Gatsby art deco-style folding board saying, 'Welcome to the roaring twenties; live now and pay later.' Black and white feathers, carefully placed in gold and silver-coloured bottles, adorn every table. Balloons and pearl string beads are used as decoration throughout the auditorium, where music is blasting at top volume. The six of us pick a table and sit down. I excuse myself to go to the bathroom. On my way there, I run into Josh and Jaimy. They're both wearing the same outfit as they did during the school play. Their black-tail coats and pin-striped trousers don't look out of place at all in this twenties extravaganza.

"Nice top hat," Josh says, pointing at my face.

"Thanks, right back at ya," I say, seeing that they have theirs on as well.

"So, uhm, Josh, I've been meaning to tell you that you did an amazing job co-directing the school play. And you too, Jaimy. The play was really good."

"Glad you enjoyed it. We did well because we were blessed with an amazing cast of actors, dancers, singers and backstage crew. To be honest, we're happy it's finished. It's been an exhausting couple of months."

"True," Jaimy adds. "We've pulled so many all-nighters; it's nice to be able to go to bed and get some actual sleep, isn't it, darling?"

Josh turns slightly red at Jaimy, mentioning them going to sleep together.

"Sure, hon, that's definitely a perk now that we're done directing. If you don't mind me asking, I saw you come in here with Lexi. Are you two dating?"

"Yep, we are; we've been going out for a couple of weeks now; she's amazing."

"I'm so happy for you, hope things will work out great for you guys."

Now it's my time to feel uncomfortable, especially since that daunting feeling I had when I pulled up on Lexi's driveway is back.

"Yeah, thanks, Josh. I was heading for the little boys' room, so see you guys later."

It's good to see that there is no resentment or hard feelings between Josh and me. We both found people we care deeply about, and this time, those feelings are mutual. I walk a little further down the hall to find an empty bathroom. I'm starting to sweat and feel as if I'm about to throw up. I walk over to the sink and splash some water on my face. As I dry my face with paper towels, I take a look in the mirror. I'm paler than usual. Maybe I'm just tired and imagining things, but I think someone else is looking back at me. I blink a few times, before I focus my eyes; I wasn't wrong; somebody else *is* staring back at me.

Jai Patel-Jones

We're back at school to store away our pride posters and signs for next year. We're all hanging out in Mr Blend's art room, and there's a serious after party going on. Bryce is playing his Spotify list at top volume, Kelly and Frida are dancing, and Paquito is raiding the vending machines for snacks and soft drinks. Mr Blend is showing his husband the latest art projects we've been working on. I've never felt more at home in this place. Yet I cannot shake off this harrowing feeling, slowly creeping up on me. At the parade, I was fine, so I might feel better after a sip of cold water. As I walk to the bathroom, I spot Yousef and Ben from the corner of my eye. They're in the science lab, deep in conversation. Just as I'm about to say hi as I walk past, Ben cups Yousef's face. Yousef leans in, and they kiss. Whoa, I'm so happy for them. Wonder if my little notes and origami roses did the trick. I wrote to both of them to meet the other one for a rendezvous after the parade. As far as I can tell, this secretly orchestrated date is going great.

I fill my water bottle at the tap. I take a few sips and wait till my stomach settles. As I'm about to leave, my head starts spinning. It's the same feeling I had when I tumbled off that bridge. I close my eyes for a few seconds, hoping the spinning will stop. As I look in the mirror, I realise that, for the first time in months, I am looking at myself again. My own face is staring back at me, not Kobe's piercing blue eyes. It's me. I take a look at my hands, but they're Kobe's. I pat my arms and chest, but it's

Kobe's muscular frame. I'm still him.

The face I see in the mirror is looking at me in confusion and surprise. This must be it; we're going back home. I close my eyes again and wait for it to happen. Until I notice, it doesn't. We're both still here, speechless, looking at ourselves in a mirror.

Kobe Dewinter and Jai Patel-Jones

"Hi, Kobe," I finally say.

"Can you hear me? 'Cause I have no idea how this works."

"Me neither, but yes, I can hear you."

"Are you all right? This is so weird."

"I suppose I'm fine under the circumstances. Nice top hat, by the way."

"Oh, thanks; I'm at a twenties school dance. Vikram and Robin picked this one out for me."

"Sounds like something my dads would definitely go for. How are they?"

"Besides squabbling over where to put the petunias and roses, they're fine."

"Oh good, I'd be worried if they didn't argue over flowers."

"I'm afraid one of these days they'll force me and Lexi to sit through a marathon of *Ground Breaking Gardening* episodes."

"You and Lexi?"

"Uhm, yes, we're dating."

"Wow, that's amazing and a little surprising, to be honest. Wouldn't think she'd be your type, judging from what I've heard about you."

"Oh God, I bet you wouldn't. Before I ended up here, I was prejudiced and a bit of a dick."

"No kidding, you certainly didn't win any popularity contests over here. I spent ages fixing your reputation and proving to everyone that you're kind, creative and capable of being a good friend. But if Lexi is into you, you must be doing something right over there."

"It helps that everyone is so nice. Your dads are amazing; it's great to be part of a loving and caring family. I became friends with Selma and Jess really fast. They're fun and easy-going. After an awkward start with Josh and Jaimy, we're good now. And Lexi has been amazing from the moment we met. She's been helping me filling in all the blanks about your life."

"Does she know who you are?"

"Yes, I've told her. She wasn't that surprised. She told me I suck at step aerobics while you are top of your class, apparently."

"*Haha*, so you survived one of David's classes at the gym?"

"Barely, I quit after half a workout. I did join the handball team, though."

"Sounds like you've made quite a life for yourself there."

"I'm really trying; how are you doing over there?"

"I've had a very rocky start. Everyone besides Roy and Jake hated me at school. Your parents were very focused on their careers, and I almost got expelled for vandalising school property."

"I'm so sorry, Jai; I know I left one heck of a mess."

"Well, at least things couldn't get any worse. I ditched Roy and Jake and started making an effort with the GSA. It took a while to earn their trust, though, especially Paquito's."

"Wait you're friends with Paquito?"

"A bit more than that; he's my boyfriend."

"Wow, he fell for you after the way I treated him?"

"Like I said, it wasn't easy, but joining the GSA really helped making new friends."

"Is that why you have those rainbow flags painted on your face?"

"We went to Pride this afternoon. It was incredible. Can't wait till next year's parade."

"Speaking of next year, have you ever thought of going back to your world?"

"All the time, but I had no idea how. So, I've been living day by day, waiting for something like this to happen."

"Same over here. I've grown very fond of everyone in this town, but I can't help but wonder if my parents are all right."

"They're fine. Your dad was hospitalised a while back. He underwent surgery, but made a full recovery. It was a wake-up call for both of your parents. They're much more focused on each other now and, well, on me too."

"Good to hear. When I left, things weren't that great."

"Kobe, this is so weird. I'm looking at my own face while I'm still you."

I stretch my arm, hoping it will bring me closer to who I once was. As I reach out, I feel the mirror's cold, smooth glass underneath my fingertips. And all of a sudden, my fingertips are brushing Kobe's face. Oh God, my arm went straight through. As I pull back, Kobe looks at me as if I've just slapped him.

"What the heck, Jai? How is this possible?"

Then, I have a sudden inkling of what might be happening.

"Kobe, stretch your arm and try touching my face."

He looks as if he's about to make a run for it.

"Come on, it won't hurt. Just do it."

Then, he slowly reaches out. His hand touches the mirror's frame. He lets it hover there for a second. Then he's cupping my face. I put my hand on his, to make sure I'm not dreaming, but I'm not. This is real. If my arm can get through that mirror, so should the rest of me.

Kobe Dewinter and Jai Patel-Jones

"Kobe, step back; I'm coming your way."

"Wait, what? Jai, be careful; you don't know what's going to happen."

"I know, but I need to find out anyway."

I pull myself up on the sink. Thank God they've done some serious maintenance since the incident that brought Kobe to my world. I'm not sure, though, how much longer this sink will hold under my weight. I grab the mirror with both hands and step through. Kobe's waiting on the other side. He grabs me around the waist and puts me down. I feel dizzy, as if I just rode a rollercoaster for the fifth time in a row. Kobe's staring at me as if he's seen a ghost. I know I haven't been working out lately, but I can't look that bad. I turn around to take a look at myself in the mirror. Oh my God, there are two of us – well actually, there are two of me. I'm me again. I'm Jai, but so is Kobe. If anyone were to walk in on us right now, they would think they'd gone insane. Or that someone spiked the punch a bit too much.

"I'm me again, and I'm back," I stammer.

"So that's what this mirror does; it's a portal. Once you cross over, you're you again. I wonder if it works both ways."

Before I can stammer another word, Kobe's on the sink; he grabs the top of the mirror with both hands as if hanging on to a horizontal bar. Then, he swings both of his legs through the glass simultaneously. He lands with a thud on the other side. When he turns around, I see that the mirror has worked both ways. Kobe is himself again.

"How do you feel, Kobe?"

"I'm fine, I guess. I'm glad to be out of that three-piece tuxedo, though. It looks way better on you. How are you holding up, Jai?"

"I'm good, and you're right about my outfit. I'm definitely rocking this top hat. But clothes aside, you know what I don't get? When we first swapped worlds, we didn't step through any mirrors. We both hit our heads and ended up with massive headaches."

"That's true, Jai. I'm in exactly the same bathroom as I was when I crossed over the first time. This mirror hit me square in the face. So, that must have been the trigger; it's a portal. Didn't you hit your head when you fell off that bridge? There must be some sort of portal down there, too."

"That makes sense, regardless of how unbelievably strange it sounds. We both fell through portals at the exact same time, causing us to swap bodies."

"What are we going to do now that we're back where we belong?"

"Let's go home to our families and friends for a bit. It's Saturday, so let's meet up here after school on Monday at five."

"Sounds like a plan, I'm in."

"Good luck, Kobe."

"Good luck, Jai."

Kobe Dewinter

So, this is it. I'm in my own room again, waiting for Mum and Dad to come home from work. I scroll through my messages. There's nothing from Roy or Jake, which is odd since we've been friends since primary school. I know Jai has been hanging out with a different crowd, but still. There is one message from Yousef Khan saying *thank you, thank you, thank you,* and a blowing kiss emoji.

No idea what that is all about. I have another one from Ben Weinberg saying, *Nice work, Cupid*, with a winky face emoji. What the heck has Jai been up to? Mum sent me a text saying she'd love to have some of that delicious tangerine duck for dinner again. Tangerine duck? I can barely fry an egg. Dad mailed me a proposal he submitted to the city council to install CCTV in our city park. Why on earth would he want that? And why do I need to know about this? I've been gone for only a few months, but it feels like I woke up from a twenty-year coma. I hardly recognise my own life. Then there's Paquito. Before I went home, I texted Jai's GSA group app. I told them I was having a bit of a headache and I'd be going home to get some rest.

Seconds after I sent my message, Paquito started texting me: *Kobe, wait, are you all right? Let me take you home. I'll stay with you till your parents get back. Will make you some hot chocolate. And tuck you in for a nice nap with benefits, winky emoji.* I haven't sent anything back. I don't mean to ghost him, but where do I even start explaining I'm not the Kobe he thinks I am? I can't pretend to be Jai and hook up with him. It's best if I avoid him for now; I'll ask Jai what to do on Monday.

I'm exhausted by the day's events. Guess I'll take a hot shower and get some sleep. I get undressed and walk into my bathroom. At least, that's where I think I am. About a dozen bottles are lined up according to colour and contents. I spot at least five different shampoos, three conditioners, body lotions, body creams, face masks, luffas, sponges, hair masks, bath salts and scented candles. Leave it up to Jai to converge my shower into a wellness spa. As I soap up with one of the bottles, I notice that my bathroom isn't the only thing he put his hands on. Down under, I'm completely bald. The only body part I've ever shaved in my life is my face. Truth be told, my junk does look bigger now, but I prefer a little shrubbery down there. I change into a clean pair of boxers. There's a pair of silk PJs on my bed and a floral-print kimono. I toss them both aside and crawl under the covers. I fall into a deep and restless sleep.

When I wake up, the house is dark and quiet. It's well past midnight. I'm wide awake, but my parents are fast asleep. Also, I'm starving. It's been ages since I've had anything to eat. I put on Jai's kimono and head downstairs. I open the fridge. It's stocked with food as usual, but something looks different. The vegetable drawers are crammed with fresh produce. There are fruit smoothies, high fibre yoghurt cups and there are lots of smoked and cured fish. Luckily, I spot some left-over tangerine duck.

As I heat up my food, I think of what I want to do this weekend. I obviously want to spend some time with my folks. Also, I'd like to reconnect with Roy and Jake. I know Jai thinks they're nothing but bullies, but I know better. We've been friends for ages.

Maybe there's even time to hit the gym for a proper workout. When I'm finished eating, I head back upstairs. I set the alarm so I can surprise my parents with a lavish breakfast. If Jai can cook tangerine duck, I should be able to manage some eggs and bacon.

As I hear my parents stumble down the stairs, I put the finishing touch on my first home-cooked breakfast. I cooked scrambled eggs, strips of fried bacon, French toast, and I made freshly squeezed orange juice. Then I clean our Barista Express coffee maker. It's all set and ready to go. Dad loves his espressos in the morning, and Mum barely speaks before she's had two latte macchiatos.

"Good morning, love; you're up early," Mum says as she saunters in.

"Morning, Kobe, what a busy bee you've been. Look at all this food."

"Uhm, yes, I thought I'd make you some breakfast since I didn't cook you any of that tangerine duck you wanted for dinner last night."

"Oh, that's all right. Your dad made a lovely quinoa salad, didn't you, darling?"

"Sure, did love. Tonight, I'm making vegan lasagna and Greek yoghurt brownies for dessert, of course, sans butter and oil."

"Oh, I can't wait; your dad's becoming quite the chef, Kobe. Can I get you a decaf cappuccino with skimmed milk?"

"If you're having one too, love, there's no need to go the extra mile for me."

"Don't be silly, darling; it's no trouble at all. I think I'll have a cup of camomile tea this morning."

Oh my God, who are these people? I think I've wandered

into the wrong house. Or did my parents fall through a portal too and swap bodies with two health nutrition enthusiasts?

"Can I get you both some scrambled eggs and bacon?"

"That looks delicious, Kobe; just the scrambled eggs for me, son."

"You love bacon, Dad, and you're not on speaking terms with anyone until you've had a few rounds of espresso. What's happened?"

"What are you talking about? You happened, Kobe. After I came back from the hospital, you put me on a health and exercise regime. Didn't like it at first, but turned out it was just what I needed. Lost quite a few pounds already, but no cheat day for me."

"And you, Mum, camomile tea?"

"Yes, darling. My yoga instructor says it cleanses my aura and relaxes my muscles at the same time. Can't start my day without it."

I feel like I'm having breakfast with Collin and Lisa rather than my own parents. Though it will probably take some getting used to his new version of them, I quite like it. They're affectionate, they're capable of having a decent conversation without grease or caffeine-induced foods, and they've embraced a more active and healthier lifestyle.

"So, what are your plans for today, Dad?"

"I have an indoor cycling class at ten. Then I'll have some work to do about a proposition I'm writing. I want to submit it to the city council first thing Monday morning."

"Does it have anything to do with the CCTV cameras you want to have installed at the city park?"

"Well, in a way, it does. After you got hate crimed there by a bunch of kids, I came up with this idea. I want every school in town to teach LGBTQ+ classes about acceptance and inclusion."

Wait, what? I got hate crimed? At the park? That's why he emailed me that proposal about those cameras.

"What about you, Mum? Any plans, or are you having a lazy Sunday?"

"Oh no, darling, I'm helping out at the food bank this morning. I have a yoga class this afternoon, but tonight is all about us. We'll have dinner and watch a movie together. It's your pick, Kobe."

"Yes, son, but please remember we've watched *The Notebook* and *Eat, Pray, Love* half a dozen times by now. So, a bit of a change might be nice."

With that, they clear their plates and head upstairs to get dressed.

Jai Patel-Jones

Here I am at a twenties school dance in a three-piece suit and matching top hat. Normally speaking, this would be the perfect night out. Now I dread going back to join my friends. But I can't stay out here for much longer; they'll wonder where I've gone. As I walk into the auditorium, I spot Lexi sitting at a table with Selma and Jess. And there are two people in yoga outfits who look suspiciously like Collin and Lisa.

"Jai, over here, where have you been?" Jess is shouting over the music as she waves at me.

"Sorry, guys, I ran into, uhm, Marty and Lucas from my handball team."

"I can imagine you had lots to discuss since the final game is next Saturday. A little birdie – well, actually, your teammate Karen told me you're playing court. Congrats, Jai; Lucas must have complete faith in you," Selma says.

"Well, yeah, I guess so. Hope I won't let them down."

"I'm sure you won't; Karen told me you're this season's big surprise."

"Believe me, I'm as surprised as she is."

"Oh my God, I love this song. Come on, Jai, let's dance."

Lexi takes me by the hand as we walk to the dance floor. Lady Gaga's Poker Face is blasting through the speakers. Half the school is on the dance floor. Collin is doing a snake-like dance move lying down on the floor, while Lisa is moonwalking around him.

Selma and Jess are holding hands, jumping up and down to the beat. This is definitely one of my favourite songs. For a moment, I forget today's unexpected turn of events and go all out on the dance floor. It's really crowded, so when the song ends, I've lost sight of Lexi. As I scan the room for her, I see Josh and Jaimy slow dancing to a Michael Bublé song. They both look stunning in their tailcoat tuxedos. I know Kobe has patched things up with Josh, but seeing them together like that still stings. I don't fancy him any more, but I would have liked the opportunity to tell him how he made me feel when I caught him cheating. Guess that's water under the bridge now. I walk over to our table, where Lexi, Collin and Lisa are drinking punch.

"Hey, hon, I got you a drink too. With all that dancing, we shouldn't forget to hydrate."

"Thanks, Lexi."

"Oh, and if you'd like to spice things up, I have a little something extra to add to your punch," Lexi says while showing a flask.

"Not for me; I'm afraid; I'm driving, remember? How about you, Collin, want to add a little extra zing?"

"Nope, though I think some almond milk would really enhance the flavour. I'll bring some next time."

"Listen, I'm a bit peckish; I'll get us some of those PB and J sandwiches I saw on the buffet."

There's a buffet table covered in sandwiches, baked goods, and other sweet and savoury treats. I spot a plate with blueberry muffins – Robin's signature snack. The school dance is catered by parents, so there's lots to choose from. I take a plate and stack sandwiches: a couple of blueberry muffins, a handful of mini quiches and two slices of pizza.

"Wow, you've really worked up an appetite on the

dancefloor."

I turn around and there's Josh, holding two plates.

"Oh, hi, Josh. This is for the entire table, although I doubt Collin will eat anything that isn't soaked in almond milk."

"I'm about to plate up for me and Jaimy. He's vegan now, so I'll have to be careful what to get him."

"I'm pretty sure my dad's muffins are vegan. He bakes them for Sunday morning town meetings, too."

"I remember your dad's muffins. The best after-school snack I've ever had. One of the perks of hanging out with you, Jai."

"Oh, right. Well, people do date me because of my dad's baking skills I've been told. Uhm, listen, there's this thing I've been wanting to tell you for a while. I know it's weird bringing this up at a school dance, especially since we've both moved on, but uh…"

"What is it, Jai?"

"We never talked about that morning when I walked in on you kissing Jaimy in the auditorium. I was utterly crushed when I saw you kiss someone else. Especially since I tried to be such a supportive boyfriend while you were dealing with all this pressure of co-directing the play."

"You're right; we should have talked about this sooner. I don't have any excuse for what I did. I was an insensitive prick, and you didn't deserve to be treated this way. I am so sorry I made you feel bad about yourself. You're an amazing guy, Jai, and hurting you like that is something I'll always regret."

"Thanks, Josh; I guess I needed to hear this to have some sort of closure."

"No problem; I should have told you this months ago."

"Well, better start filling up that plate before all the vegan muffins are gone."

I will. Have a great night, Jai."

As I walk back to our table, a weight has been lifted from my shoulders. Now, I can move on for real.

As I pull up onto Lexi's driveway, I'm suddenly aware that we're supposed to be more than just friends. Collin and Lisa get out of the car as soon as I've parked. Lexi takes my hand and is looking at me.

"That was a great night. Can't remember the last time I had this much fun. Not sure I want it to end. My parents won't mind if you're staying over again."

"Oh, well, I'd love to, Lexi. It's just that I promised my dad I'd help out in the garden tomorrow morning. You know how worked up Vikram can get over where to put the petunias."

"Oh, of course, I know how passionate they are about gardening. Perhaps I'll swing by tomorrow to make sure Robin hasn't bludgeoned Vikram with a shovel."

"*Haha*, yep, I better hide the shears."

I open Lexi's door. Before she gets out, she leans in and kisses me. Oh crap, what am I supposed to do now? I'm not who she thinks I am, but I can't tell her Kobe has left. I lean in and kiss her back. While we kiss, I can't help thinking about Paquito. His soft lips, his cute button-shaped nose, his musky scent and his soft, dark curls. I miss him and wish he were here.

I tiptoe into the living room; Vikram and Robin are probably fast asleep. As I'm about to walk upstairs, someone flips on the lights.

"Darling, how was your night? Robin and I wanted to stay up to hear all about your evening. I'm afraid we dozed off just before you came in."

"Sorry to wake you. I had a wonderful night and..." Then I choke up. I haven't seen my dads for months, but it feels so good to be home again.

"Love, are you all right?" Robin says, while rubbing his eyes.

"I'm fine, really; it's just been a long night. I ran into Josh and had a little heart-to-heart with him. Finally, got to say how he made me feel when he hooked up with Jaimy."

"Darling, that's very brave of you. Hope it helped you move on."

"It did. Actually, we're good now. Thanks for staying up, but I'm exhausted, to be honest. Think I'm going to turn in."

"That's all right, love. Goodnight."

As I head upstairs, Vikram and Robin have started watching reruns of *Ground Breaking Gardening*. Better persuade them to do some actual gardening tomorrow. What if Lexi drops by, and we're not knee-deep in the dirt? She'll know that I lied to her.

My room is in pretty much the same state it was, when I left. Only there's a drum kit in the corner. I'm dying to know how Kobe convinced my dads to let him have this in his bedroom. They hate loud musical instruments. I take off my three-piece suit and go for a quick shower.

Although Kobe's muscular physique certainly has its merits, it feels good to be in my own skin again. My calves have really bulked up, though, probably thanks to all those handball practices. I grab a razor and hit the shower. For all that Kobe's worth, he's a stranger to manscaping.

Kobe Dewinter

After I've cleared the table, I get dressed. My wardrobe hasn't changed much apart from three pairs of chinos, a couple of fancy shirts and a pair of suede loafers. Luckily, I spot a clean pair of jeans and my favourite hoodie. I text Jake and Roy to see if they want to hang out. 'Message not delivered,' it says. Did they change their number? Oddly, they didn't tell me. You know what? I'll just drop by. Jake lives two blocks away, and Roy is usually at his place. I grab my coat and head out.

As I ring the doorbell, I scroll through my messages. Paquito has sent me another half-dozen. Is he obsessed with me or something? He keeps asking how I'm doing and whether I have any plans for today. Also, he keeps texting me eggplant and sausage emojis. What on earth has Jai been up to? I'm about to ring the bell again when an upstairs window opens. It's Jake.

"Hey, Jake, what's up?"

"What are you doing here?"

"Just checking in, feels like ages since we hung out."

"Why should we, you almost got us expelled, you dick."

Wait, I did what? Then Roy appears next to Jake.

"Hey, Kobe, shouldn't you be with your boyfriend Pussyto?"

"What's going on, you guys? We've been friends since forever. Can't we hang out like old times?"

"Wait up, let me get the door for you," Roy says.

Oh great, they've come around. I knew we'd still be friends.

As I wait for Roy to get to the door, I look up at Jake. As I squint my eyes against the sunlight, a huge stream of cold water splashes all over me. I'm soaking wet.

"There you go, you little narc; that's all you'll ever get from us," Roy shouts while showing an empty bucket.

"Now piss off, Kobe; go find your rainbow flag-infested friends."

I can't believe this; Paquito was right. They're horrible.

While I park my bike in our driveway, I hear someone calling out for me.

"Kobe, wait, it's me."

Paquito pops up, holding a wicker basket with what looks like soup.

"I brought you some treats to make you feel b... What the heck, why are you drenched?"

Suddenly, I feel emotionally drained. I can't even speak, afraid I might actually burst into tears. Paquito wraps me in his arms and gives me a hug.

"It's all right. Don't worry, let's get you some dry clothes."

He takes me gently by the arm and steers me into the house, up the stairs to my room. He grabs a towel so I can dry my face. Then he looks at my wardrobe and picks a pair of green chinos and a blue and white striped shirt. Remember this, Kobe? You wore this outfit the first time you came round to my place. I'm still shaking, so I change in front of Paquito without thinking twice. He doesn't seem disturbed in the slightest. In fact, he helps me dress by buttoning up my shirt. He smooths out a few crinkles and creases by stroking his hands all over the fabric, caressing my arms, my back, my chest and my shoulders. He inches closer and closer; I can feel his warm breath on my face. Then his lips are on mine. I'm at a loss for what to do next. He can't find out that I'm not the Kobe he hooked up with. So, I do what Jai would have done and kiss him back. Only a few months ago, I was vandalising rainbow flags and harassing queer kids at school. Now, I am kissing a boy for the first time in my life. His lips are soft and taste like vanilla; his kisses are slow and deep. I can't stop thinking about Lexi, though. Her kisses are passionate and quick, as if she's constantly afraid we're running out of time.

Her breath has this sweet, fruity scent to it, like strawberry jelly donuts. How I wish she'd be here with me right now.

Paquito has stopped kissing me and looks at me long and hard. He takes off his glasses and polishes them with the hem of his shirt. He puts them back on and takes me in one more time.

"Is everything all right, Paquito?"

"Who are you?"

"What do you mean? I'm Kobe, your boyfriend."

"No, you're not. The Kobe I know feels, smells and acts totally different than you. Not to mention the kissing."

I'm starting to feel a little miffed now.

"What about the kissing, not good enough?"

"It was nice, just not how you usually kiss me."

"Look, I'm sorry if I'm not up to your usual standards."

"That's not it; it just feels like I'm kissing a totally different person."

That's when I decide to tell him the truth, 'cause deep down inside, he already knows.

"You're right; you are kissing someone else. I am Kobe, but the guy you've been dating is called Jai."

"Wait, what? Do you have some identical twin I don't know about?"

"It's a little more complicated than that. So, please hear me out."

I tell him all about our incredible body swap journey so far. When I'm finished, he stays quiet for a while.

"I understand if you don't believe me. I hardly do myself, and I'm the one living it."

"I believe you, Kobe. To be honest, it all makes so much more sense now. One day, you're a bully; the next day, you come to my rescue like a knight in shining armour. You join the GSA, which you despised, you show some serious origami skills at the fundraiser, and you were epic at Pride."

"When I was in Jai's world, I learned a lot about unconditional love, true friendship and how wonderful it is to be yourself without any prejudice or judgement from others. It changed me; I'm not that insensitive jerk you knew before you met Jai. I know it's a little late, but uhm, I'm sorry for everything I put you through. You're a great guy, and Jai's lucky to have you."

"Well, better late than never. I can see you've changed. The Kobe I knew would have never kissed a boy just to have someone's back."

"Sorry you had to endure that."

"Speaking of endurance, you looked like you were having a rough morning when I ran into you on the driveway."

"I went over to Jake's. He and Roy gave me the cold shoulder, or, to be more precise, a cold shower."

"Why would you even want to hang out with those delinquents after what they did to you? Oh, wait, that happened to Jai. They locked him up in a storage closet. Left him there gagged and bound with rainbow flags."

Oh my God, this keeps getting darker by the minute. Can't believe Jai survived here this long. Thank goodness he had the GSA and Paquito to look after him.

"So, is Jai coming back on Monday?"

"I really don't know. If we're swapping worlds, we'd be giving up our family and friends, but if we stay, we'd lose the ones we love."

"You think he loves me?"

"He'd be crazy not to."

"Weird question, but can I come with you when you see him? If Jai decides to stay where he is, well, at least I get to say goodbye."

"Of course, as long as you don't tell anyone else."

"Have you thought about what you want?"

"All the time, I'm just not sure yet."

Jai Patel-Jones

I wake up to the all-too-familiar bustle of Robin making breakfast and Vikram chatting his ear off. I have one more day to decide where I belong. I can't help wondering what it would be like to never see my dads again. At least they'd have Kobe for a son. As far as I can tell, he's done a pretty decent job. But if I stay, I will never get to see Paquito again. Oh great, now I'm blinking tears away. This is ridiculous; we've only been dating for a couple of months. Still, I feel like half of me is missing without him by my side. I didn't even get to say goodbye when I left; it all happened so fast. I'm just going to have to put my emotions on hold for a little while longer. I can't risk my dads getting suspicious.

"There you are, sleepy head. Good morning."

"Morning, Dad; morning, Pops."

"You look exhausted. Didn't you sleep well?"

"I'm fine; it's just that I've had a lot on my plate lately."

"I understand, darling. Is everything all right with Lexi? We thought you'd be staying over there after the dance. We were quite surprised when you texted us you were coming home."

"Oh, uhm, we're fine. Just really needed to get some sleep. Have to be in top shape for next week's game."

"Wow, Jai, you've turned into quite the athlete, hasn't he, Vikram? Only a few months ago, you were all about step aerobics, and look at you now. We're so proud of you, honey."

"Thanks, pops, but we haven't won yet."

"So, what are your plans for today?"

"Lexi might visit; she said she'd be happy to help out in the garden."

"Oh, that's very sweet of her, but you kids should enjoy your day doing stuff you actually like. Can't imagine having to listen to our constant bickering is very inspiring. And besides, it's Sunday morning. Aren't you two coming to town meeting? I'm nearly done with my first batch of muffins; I made lemon curd instead of blueberry."

"Smells delicious, Pops, but I think I'll skip this week's Kiki."

"That's all right, love. Get some more rest and take it easy today. I'll leave you a couple of muffins should Lexi drop by."

After Vikram and Robin have left, I scroll through my messages. Selma texted me a hungover bed-fie with her and Jess captioned, 'Glad the twenties are behind us.' Guess Lexi's little flask became quite the hit with those two. Collin texted me about the healing powers of acidophilus milk, and promised to bring some on Monday. Great, just as I thought we were passed the almond milk phase. There's nothing from Lexi, though. I might as well keep myself busy. I'll surprise Vikram and Robin by doing some weeding in the garden. I put on a pair of garden gloves and get to work. Thanks to my dads perfectionism and countless episodes of *Ground Breaking Gardening*, there isn't much to do. I rake a couple of stray leaves and dump them in our organic waste bin.

"Thought I would find you out here."

I turn around to see Lexi leaning over our garden fence.

"Hey, Lexi, guess you weren't up for town meeting this morning either."

"Nope, my parents went, though. Collin insisted on bringing a jug of acidophilus milk to go with Mum's freshly baked chocolate chip cookies. Don't think it'll be a big hit on today's buffet."

"At least we dodged that bullet. It's too bad he's bringing some of it to school tomorrow."

"Let's make sure we give him a wide berth at lunch."

Lexi has walked up to me and holds my gloved hands in hers. She gives me a kiss and strokes my hair.

"Fancy a walk?"

"Sure, let me put my gloves and rake in the shed. Do you have anywhere in particular you want to go?"

"No, let's just walk around the block for a while. It's always so nice and peaceful, with everyone gone to town meeting."

We head out and walk in silence for a while. Then Lexi clears her throat.

"Do you think Kobe's ever coming back?"

I freeze up; oh no, she's on to me.

"What are you talking about? I'm right here."

"Cut the crap. Jai, I know it's you; I've known since last night."

It's no use keeping up appearances now.

"How did you find out?"

"I've had a hunch ever since you came back from the bathroom at the dance. There was something different about you. The way you talked and moved, you reminded me so much of, well, *you*."

"Can't believe I messed up that fast."

"It's not just that; I saw you talking to Josh for quite a while. It seemed like a serious conversation. Kobe had moved on a while ago. And when you dropped me off, you didn't want to stay over. Then we kissed, and I knew for sure. I've had enough make-out sessions with Kobe to know that wasn't him.

"Never thought my lips would give me away, but yes, it's me, Jai. I'm back."

"What brought you back?"

"The mirror that hit Kobe over the head before he woke up here, turned out to be some sort of portal. Apparently, there's one at our school as well. We both ended up there yesterday. When we looked in the mirror, we were able to see and talk to each other. I think we're somehow connected through our body swap.

It was so surreal talking to the guy whose body I inhabited for months and whose life I lived. We decided to return home for a while and discuss any further plans on Monday after school."

"I can't believe Kobe didn't say goodbye."

"It all happened so fast, Lexi; we were terrified someone would walk in on us."

"So, what will you guys do on Monday?"

"I have honestly no idea."

Kobe Dewinter

Monday goes by in a haze. Paquito doesn't stray far from my side, as if he's afraid I might bail out on him. I haven't heard a thing any teacher said in class today. During break time I haven't so much as looked at my lunch box. At one point, Paquito worries I might pass out due to lack of sustenance, so he forces me to drink some apple juice. We just had our last class, Art with Mr Blend. He kept on yapping about origami flowers and our next fundraiser. I agreed to anything he asked me, just to get him out of my hair. Of course, I don't know anything about origami, so I help Yousef with his diorama about last Saturday's Pride march. After class, we head to the library. We both agreed it would be best to keep a low profile until five. Most kids go straight home when school's out, so we have the place to ourselves. Paquito finds a book to read, and soon, he's totally engrossed. I'm reading a comic, but I have to go over every sentence at least three times before it sticks. At a quarter to five, we walk up to the bathroom, where it all began. The school is open to students until five. Our janitor, Mr Fairview, is doing a final sweep around the place to make sure no one overstays their welcome. We stay well out of sight, but then we're here at last. I walk up to the sink in the middle. Jai isn't there yet; all we can do now is wait.

Jai Patel-Jones

Leaving home for what might be the last time is really difficult. I drag out breakfast as long as I can until Vikram says I'm running late. I give them both a hug before I leave, something I usually don't do.

Lexi is waiting for me in the driveway. We drive to school in silence. I sit through all of my classes without taking anything in. At lunchtime, I even try some of Collin's acidophilus milk, because I haven't got the heart to tell him no. This could be my last day here, not just with Vikram and Robin, but also with my friends, my classmates, my teachers and everything else I hold dear in my world.

At the same time, I can't wait to get out of here. I miss spending time with the GSA and all of my friends; I miss Mr Blend's art class; I miss Kobe's parents; but most of all, I miss Paquito. Longing for him doesn't seem to do justice to how I feel about him. I don't just miss him; I'm pining for him.

After school, Lexi and I head over to the auditorium. We find a quiet corner to sit and wait till it's time to go. Lexi has been unusually quiet. I get it; she's missed Kobe and fears he might choose to stay where he is. When I try talking about it, she just shrugs her shoulders as if it doesn't affect her. But I see a crippling fear in her eyes, which breaks my heart. When it's a quarter to five, we get up simultaneously and find the bathroom with the mirror portal. As I open the door and scan the room, something doesn't add up. This is not the right one. All the sinks and mirrors have been removed. I turn around and face Lexi.

"I think we're in the wrong bathroom; there were sinks and mirrors last Saturday."

As we're about to leave, Mr Casey, our janitor, walks in.

"Oi, what are you lot doing in here? This bathroom is out of order; we're renovating."

"What happened to the sinks and mirrors?" Lexi asks, trying to sound calm.

"We've chucked them out; the sinks were leaking, and the mirrors needed replacement."

Oh no, the portal's gone. I walk up to the wall where only two days ago, I stepped through a mirror. I touch the bare tiles, but nothing. Not a hint of a portal or any other doorway to Kobe's world. I begin to sweat and try hard not to freak out."

"Take it easy, son; this bathroom will be right as rain in a week or so," Mr Casey says.

"Thanks, Mr Casey; we'll find another one."

Lexi grabs my elbow and steers me to an empty classroom.

"What do we do now? Oh my God, the portal is gone. Kobe is waiting for me on the other side."

"Calm down, Jai, let's think for a minute. Didn't you tell me you woke up in his world after you fell down that bridge in the park? That means there must be another portal at the park."

"What would I do without you, Lexi? Let's go."

We storm out and run to my car. My hands are shaking so badly that Lexi's driving. Hope we're not too late. What if Kobe thinks I stood him up because I decided I wanted to stay here? Oh God, I hope he's still there.

Kobe Dewinter

It's a quarter past five, and there's still no sign of Jai. What if he decided to stay over there and couldn't bear to tell me, or say goodbye to Paquito.

"Are you sure we're in the right bathroom?" Paquito asks for the twelfth time.

"Yes, we are; it's really here. I don't know what's keeping him so long."

"What if he changed his mind and isn't coming back at all?" Paquito says quietly.

"I don't think he would do that; it doesn't sound like him at all."

At five thirty, I give up. I climb on the sink and touch the mirror with both hands. Nothing… I guess it only works when we're both there.

"What on earth do you think you're doing, Mr DeWinter?"

Mr Fairview is standing in the doorway. His face is a deep shade of red, and he is shaking with anger.

Before I can say anything to explain myself, he drones on.

"You're wrecking the place again? I know you have the principle wrapped around your little finger, but I know better. I have figured you out just fine. You're lucky Mr Calhoon is out; otherwise, it would have been a one-way ticket over there for both of you. I'll make sure you have a date with him first thing in the morning. Now get out!"

Paquito and I leave as quickly as we can. Mr Fairview

follows us all the way to the exit to make sure we leave the premises. Once we're outside, he bangs the door shut and locks up after us.

"Oh no, this cannot be happening. I have no chance of seeing Jai without that portal."

Paquito is white as a sheet, and for a moment, I think he lost the ability to speak. Then he smiles at me and grabs my arm.

"I just thought of something. Mr Blend always leaves a window open in his classroom. I noticed he forgets to close it after school. We just have to wait until Mr Fairview has left. Then we'll head straight back in."

"That's called breaking and entering, which is punishable by law."

"Have you got a better idea?"

"I don't. You're right; it's the only way to see Jai. We have to give it another shot."

"Great, let's do this."

Jai Patel-Jones

When we arrive at the park, I bolt from the car while Lexi is still parking. The sun is almost down. The park is quiet and deserted. We run to the bridge as fast as we can. I look down at the water below. This is where it all started and where it might end if we can't find that portal.

"I don't think it's up here, Jai; we should climb down and see if we can find anything."

So now we're standing under the bridge, on the riverbank.

"I have no idea what to look for; it can't be a mirror I fell through."

"Have you got any memory of hitting your head on something?"

"Nope, I just remember waking up in a bathroom at Kobe's school."

We both scan the riverbank for anything that could possibly function as a portal. Besides some twigs, leaves and stones, there's nothing here but sand. I sit down with my head resting on my knees. A surge of panic is creeping up on me again. What if this is it? What if it all ends here for good?

I'm staring at the river, praying for that portal to appear out of thin air. Then I see something flickering in the water. It looks like a large boulder about ten feet in diameter. I don't bother taking my shoes off. The water is freezing cold, but all I can think of is being too late for our meet-up. Lexi is right behind me. Together, we pick up the rock and haul it back to the riverside.

We both hoover over it, but that strange flickering light I saw a minute ago is gone. It's just a boulder. I saw what I wanted to see out of sheer despair. There's nothing here that can bring me back to Paquito. I sit down and feel my heart shatter into a million pieces.

Kobe Dewinter

"Come on, give me a leg-up."

We waited for Mr Fairview to head out, before we embarked on our little queer quest, as Paquito likes to call it. Our janitor is usually the last one to leave, so we should go unnoticed. I can't believe I'm doing this. Paquito is halfway through the window of Mr Blend's classroom. Turned out he was right. Mr Blend left the window open just enough for him to squeeze through. I silently pray our unconventional entrance isn't going to set off any alarm. There is no way I'd be able to explain this to Mr Calhoon, let alone my parents. Paquito has landed with both feet on the ground. We keep quiet for a moment, so far so good. I pull myself up on the window's ledge and crawl in after Paquito. He's opened the window a bit more, so I can pass through. As we walk to the bathroom, I consider our odds of succeeding. They seem slim to nothing. I walk up to the mirror for the second time today. There's no sign of Jai. Paquito is on edge too; his fingertips go over every square inch of that mirror. In a desperate attempt to find Jai, he calls out his name. There's not so much as a squeak from the other side.

Jai Patel-Jones

Here we are. Soaking wet from the waist down, sitting next to a plain rock underneath a bridge. I'm starting to think I completely lost it. At this point, I'm seriously starting to doubt my sanity. What if I've imagined all of it? I hit my head pretty hard when I fell off that bridge. What if it triggered some sort of hidden personality? One that believed he's Kobe, a sporty, straight guy with a bit of an attitude. That means Paquito never really existed, but in my own head. A figment of my imagination. But it felt so real. The conversations we had, the jokes we shared, the hugs, the kisses and the dates we've been on. What if my brain created an imaginary boyfriend to cope with losing my actual one, Josh? Meanwhile, I was hooking up with Lexi as my alter ego, Kobe. I can't believe the mess I've caused and the hurt that will undoubtedly follow. I feel horrible about dragging Lexi into all of this. Tears are streaming down my face. Lexi has scooched over and holds me tight. Great, I'm hearing things again. Paquito's voice is calling for me, which I realise by now, is impossible.

"Jai, I can hear someone calling your name."

Wait what? Lexi is hearing this, too? The sound is coming from that blasted rock we hauled from the river. We both look at it, and to my amazement, it lights up again. I pick up the rock and place it against a nearby tree. It is covered in dirt. I use my hands and my shirt to wipe it clean. The rock is translucent; it kind of looks like a mirror.

"Hello, anyone there?" I call out.
"Jai, it's me, Paquito, where are you?"
I'm stunned. We did find that portal after all, and it works.

Kobe Dewinter and Jai Patel-Jones

Oh my God, I can hear Paquito; he's here; they made it. I grab the rock with both hands. Lexi holds on to the hem of my shirt as if afraid I might dive straight through, which is exactly what I feel like doing.

"Be careful, Jai; don't do anything rash."

She's right; I have to be cautious. I stretch out my hand and touch the rock carefully. Its radiant glow casts sparkles all over my hand. Then it's gone. Lexi gasps. Before I can pull back my hand, I feel someone tug on the other side.

"Jai, it's me, Paquito. Can you feel my hand?"

"Yes, I can. Hold on tight."

I grab Paquito's hand and start pulling. I hear Kobe telling him to get on the sink and not let go of my hand. Then he's here.

Paquito is standing right in front of me, dark curls plastered to his forehead and a bewildered look in his eyes. But he's here, and that's all that matters. I fling my arms around him and don't let go.

After what seems like forever, Paquito pulls away. He looks at me as if he's never met me before. Of course, because he hasn't! He knows me as Kobe, not as a slender-built Indian boy who's been sobbing on his shoulder for the past five minutes. I give him some space so he can take me in.

"Hey, you," I say.

"Hi, is it really you, Kobe? I mean, Jai?"

"I'm afraid it is; it must be a bit of a shock, though."

"Believe me, after the day I've had, I'm ready to believe just about anything."

"This is what I look like in my world. Nice to meet you, by the way. I'm Jai Patel-Jones."

"Yes, Kobe told me as much."

"Paquito, I'm so sorry I didn't tell you. I was going to after Pride, but when I went to the bathroom, everything happened so fast. Before I knew, I was back home again."

"I know; Kobe explained everything to me."

"Are you mad at me?"

"To be honest, I don't know what I am; it's just a lot to process."

"Kobe, are you there?"

Lexi is on all fours, talking to the rock. "I'm right here, Lex. I think I'll stay over here for now. Last time I crossed over, I changed into Jai straight away. Can't risk having to explain Jai and his identical twin to anyone who happens to walk by."

We're all huddled around the rock as if we're Cub Scouts at a campfire.

"I'm sorry we're late. The portal in our school's bathroom is gone. They're renovating and all the mirrors have been removed. Lexi reminded me of the second portal, somewhere under this bridge. It just took us a while to find it."

"That's okay; we had a bit of bad luck ourselves. The janitor threw us out, and it took some time before we were able to sneak back in."

"So, what do we do now?"

"Lexi, I missed you so much, and I'm sorry I didn't give you a heads-up before I left."

"I figured out in no time that Jai wasn't you."

"Of course you did, hon; I didn't expect anything less from you. I understand if you're upset with me."

"Upset? I'm not upset, Kobe; I'm livid. But I missed you too."

"I don't know what the future has in store for us, Lex, or whether we'll still be together by next month. All I know is that I want to be with you for any period of time."

"Me too, Kobe, and besides, Lucas will be heartbroken if you don't make it to Saturday's game."

"What about you, Jai? Have you thought about what you want?" Kobe asks me.

I look at Paquito and grab both of his hands.

"When I first came to your world, I was confused, scared, sad, but most of all lonely. Then I met you. As Kobe, I fought so hard to earn your trust, your friendship and your affection. And it was worth it every damn step of the way. I know we've only been dating for a couple of months, but I can't think of a world where you're not by my side. So, if you'll still have me, I'd love to come home with you."

Paquito looks at me and is awfully quiet. Then he cups my face and kisses me. I'm so relieved, I start crying again.

"Hold on, lovebirds," Lexi interrupts. If Jai is going back with Paquito and Kobe's coming over here, we need to find a way to stay in touch. I mean, we do have this rock, and then there's that mirror at Kobe's school. But what if they replace it, like they did at our school?"

"I might have an idea; I'll be gone for a second. Wait for me."

Before we can put in another word, he's gone.

"Hey guys, I'm back. Look what I got you."

His hand reaches through the portal.

"Take the hammer."

"And what exactly do you want us to do with that?" Lexi asks.

"I was just thinking, wouldn't it be great if we both had one-half of that rock? If we break it, we can each keep one part. This way, we won't have to worry about bathrooms being renovated and mirrors disappearing."

"That sounds great, Kobe, but how are we going to split this rock in half? What if we accidentally smash it into a million pieces, or what if it won't break at all?" Paquito asks.

"I don't think the portal is that strong and solid. It has to be flexible, or else it wouldn't be able to let anyone through."

No matter how much I want to believe in Kobe's theory, I doubt it will work. But we're running out of options and time.

"Okay, but let's swap world's first Kobe. If it doesn't work, at least no one will be stuck in the wrong place."

I take Paquito by the hand as I step through the portal. Kobe's waiting on the other side, helping us down from the sink. Paquito sniggers.

"Well, look at that; there are two of you now. I think that's more than I can handle."

Then Kobe pulls himself up on the sink, looks back one more time, and waves at us. Then he's gone. Lexi is waiting for him on the other side.

"Honey, I'm home."

"Very funny, Kobe." But she smiles as they hug.

"Now, let's get to work; we have a portal to smash."

"Guys, wait a second. I might have a better idea." Jai calls through the portal. I'm not at all happy about you smashing that rock. If that goes south, we're done for. "I just thought of something else. What if we swap this mirror for an actual one? Then I'll take the portal home with me. You guys take that rock, and we can all keep in touch."

"Sounds like a great plan, but how are you going to swap that mirror without anyone noticing? And with anyone, I mean Mr Fairview in particular. He's already got in for you, Jai. Especially since he caught you standing on that sink after school."

"I'm not saying it will be easy, but it's worth trying. If it doesn't work, we can always decide to smash that rock. Just give me a week so I can find an identical mirror and smooth things over with Fairview and Mr Calhoon."

"Suppose it's a date then. We'll see each other one week from now, at the same time, hopefully, in a different place," Lexi says.

"Good luck, Jai," Kobe chimes in.

"Thanks guys; see you in a bit."

Kobe Dewinter

I can't believe I'm back with Lexi again. I realise she isn't the only one I've missed. I am looking forward to coming home to Vikram and Robin. They're amazing dads, and I've even missed their endless bickering over petunias and roses. I'd love to catch up with my friends Selma and Jess, and even Collin and Lisa have become important people in my life. And as I understand it, I'm expected to play a game this Saturday. Hopefully, I can pick up right where I left off.

"It's really getting late, Kobe; let's get this rock home safely."

I carry the rock to Jai's car. Luckily, Lexi held on to the keys when she drove there.

"Would you like to come home with me?"

"Are you kidding me? of course! Can't wait for you to tell me what you've been up to over there."

As we drive home, I start telling her about how my parents have changed since Jai came into their lives. I tell her about not being able to reconnect with my old friends, but having gained a colourful group of new ones called the GSA. Lexi listens and asks questions about my other life. When we pull up to my house, she looks at me.

"Sounds like you left a wonderful life behind."

"I did, but I'm getting an even better one in return because you're in it."

"Oh my God, you're so cliché, Kobe." But she cups my face

and kisses me.

Back home, Lexi goes straight up to my room to stash the rock in the back of my wardrobe. Meanwhile, I'm chatting with Vikram and Robin about my day, which is obviously a different version than what actually happened.

"Hey, Vikram and Robin. Nice to see you again."

Lexi has joined us in the living room.

"Hey Lexi, how are you? So great to have you over. Vikram and I already ate, but let me heat you up some tater tot casserole. I'll bet you kids are ravenous."

"Thanks, Pops; sounds delicious."

After dinner, we catch up with my dads. Lexi admires their garden elaborately, which results in the four of us watching a few episodes of *Ground Breaking Gardening*. Back upstairs, we check to see if the rock is still there. Lexi wrapped it in one of my old shirts and stashed it underneath my aerobics gear.

"Don't think you'll be using that outfit anytime soon."

She's right about that. I carefully unwrap the rock. Looking at it closely for the first time, it looks like any other plain old boulder, except it's translucent. It doesn't light up any more, which means that Jai and Paquito have left, too.

"You know what I just realised?"

"What is it, Kobe?"

"I've got my very own version of Narnia up here in my bedroom. A wardrobe that contains a portal to another world. How weird is that? All we need is a lion and a witch."

"You do remind me a bit of Edmund. Didn't he end up with that handsome-looking centaur, Glenstorm?"

Wait, what? Wow, leave it up to this world to make Narnia even more queer. Not that I would ever say that out loud. I've changed, so same-sex interspecies relationships are perfectly acceptable as far as I'm concerned.

"I recall the story a bit differently, but there were definitely some centaurs and a boy named Edmund in it."

We carefully place the rock at the back of my wardrobe. I'm not the least bit worried about Vikram and Robin finding out; they would never go through my stuff.

"So, have you got any idea what you want to do after you graduate? I know I've asked this before, but back then, you didn't know you were going to stick around."

"I haven't given it any thought yet with all that's been going on. I used to have my mind set on travelling. Getting as far away from my parents and my hometown as possible."

"You could still travel if that's what you want."

"Don't think I could miss you again, Lexi."

"Oh, look who's gone all soft now. Supposed I could take a gap year and join you."

"That would be awesome – exploring this colourful world together. After that, I'd like to go to college. Maybe train to be a handball coach or something. I think I really got the hang of it."

"You sure did; Lucas wouldn't hesitate to write you a letter of recommendation."

"So, Lexi, the night I disappeared, we were at that twenties dance at school. But I never got to ask you for a dance."

I get up, take a bow, and offer her my hand.

"If you will, my lady."

"I most certainly do." Lexi giggles and takes my hand.

Instead of a Charleston, I put on some slow music. I escort her to the middle of my room. We hold on to each other tightly while swaying to the music.

I never want this song to end, and I never want to be without Lexi again. After the song is finished, we snuggle up under the covers. I can't believe my luck and hope with all my heart this is our happily ever after.

Jai Patel-Jones

As soon as we step through the portal, I come up with a plan. We obviously can't remove the mirror and take it with us right now. We would be first on Mr Fairview's list of suspects. Instead, I take a picture so I can find one that looks exactly like it. We crawl out the same way Kobe and Paquito came in, through an open window in the art room. Hopefully, our little escapade didn't set off the alarm. I think we're good, though, 'cause there's no sign of the police. Once we've left the school grounds, I breathe a sigh of relief. Mission accomplished, I'm back where it all started, and most importantly, I'm back with Paquito.

"So, uhm, would you like to come over to my place?"

"Sure, let me just text my parents that I'm staying over. I told them earlier I was having dinner at your place, so this shouldn't come as a surprise."

We cycle back in silence. Although we're both happy to be in each other's lives again, we haven't talked things through yet. After all, I left without saying goodbye, not knowing when or if I'd ever come back.

My parents have already eaten. They're watching an old sitcom on the telly. We're not in the mood for dinner, but I feel like I need to keep myself busy, anyway.

"I never got you that dessert I was going to make before I ended up in the hospital. Think I might still have the ingredients. As I roam around the kitchen trying to whip up a long-overdue dessert, Paquito brings me up to date on any school gossip I've missed.

"Ben and Yousef have been going strong for weeks now. They're even planning their first trip together during the summer holidays. And Kelly's got this internship at her favourite nail salon; she won't shut up about it. Of course, we're all happy for her."

Finally, my dessert is ready. The lava cakes come out looking just like the picture in my recipe book. They're still oven-warm and filled with dark liquid chocolate, which slowly seeps out once we dig in. This is definitely a great peace offering. Paquito is actually eating with his eyes closed, savouring every bite. When we're finished, we tell my parents goodnight and head upstairs. I'm not sure if all is right between us, 'cause Paquito has gone awfully quiet again.

I walk up to him and wrap my arms around him. Paquito stands perfectly still, and for a moment, I think he isn't going to hug me back. Then he picks me up and throws me on the bed. I've barely landed on my back when he flips me over. I'm about to suggest we take our clothes off when he slaps my backside.

"What the heck?" I shout.

"This is for leaving me behind without so much as saying goodbye. I was worried sick about you; don't you ever do that to me again."

I sit up but lie back down straight away 'cause, boy, does that sting.

"I'm so sorry for what I've put you through; I promise it won't happen again."

"You're lucky those lava cakes were delicious; I was holding back."

"You're kidding me, right? Can't even sit up."

"Then why don't you stay down and let me see if I can ease

the pain."

While I lie on my belly, Paquito slowly takes off my shirt, my socks and my pants until I'm in nothing but my birthday suit. Just as in the hospital, he starts kissing me from the neck down. I grab the sheets, failing to suppress some awkward guttural sounds. When he's all the way down, the sting has mostly worn off. I turn around and pull his shirt over his head. He steps out of his pants and flings his boxers into a corner. He tells me to get on all fours. I hear him rummage through my drawers with condoms and lube.

"Would you like a happy ending?" he asks me.

"Yes, and a messy one, too," I reply.

And that is exactly what I get.

Kobe Dewinter

I can't believe it's been a week. Today, we'll find out if Jai and Paquito successfully switched that mirror. Lexi and I are both sitting on the floor in front of my wardrobe. We've unwrapped the rock, polished it for good measure, and are now waiting for an incoming message from the other side. Lexi seems nervous; she can't stop fidgeting.

"Why are they late? What if something happened like last time?"

"Don't worry, Lexi, it's not even ten to five. I'm sure they'll make it."

As if on cue, the rock starts to light up.

"Hello, anyone there?"

"Oh my God, it's Jai; they're here," Lexi says.

As we both stare at the rock, Jai and Paquito slowly come into focus. They're in Jai's bedroom.

"Hey, you guys, how are you?"

"We're fine, Kobe. Pulled off a little stunt this week, switching those mirrors."

"How did you manage that?"

"Well, Jai came up with this insane plan that could have gotten us both expelled and possibly jailed."

"But it didn't, darling. I went shopping for a mirror identical to the portal at school. Wasn't easy, but eventually, I found one close enough to resemble the original. On Thursday; Paquito called in sick on purpose. Just after lunch, I pulled the fire alarm in the science lab. The whole school had to evacuate. I ran to the bathroom and snatched the mirror from the wall.

Paquito was waiting for me with the substitute mirror outside that open window in Mr Blend's art room. By now, most students had left the building. I still had to be careful to avoid any emergency response staff scouring the premises for students left behind. I made it to the bathroom without getting caught. I hung the mirror, turned around, and of course, there was Mr Fairview in a high vis jacket looking furious as usual."

"No, he wasn't." Lexi and I both gasp.

"Yep, he was. Since I was in a bathroom, it wasn't that difficult to come up with an excuse for not having left yet."

"Getting the portal home was quite a challenge, too," Paquito continues.

"Try sneaking out with a mirror in your hands and hundreds of students swarming the school grounds during an evacuation, while everyone thinks you're at home. Luckily, I brought this huge backpack I borrowed from a cousin of mine. So, I stuffed the mirror in it, covered my head with one of Jai's hoodies, and tried to blend in. At the first opportunity, I snuck out and ran home."

"You guys rock so hard," Lexi says.

"Really impressive," I add.

"Thanks; teamwork makes the dream work, I suppose," Jai smiles. "Speaking of teamwork, is that a trophy I see in your room?"

"Yes, it is. We won last Saturday's game and can call ourselves regional champions for a whole year."

"Kobe was epic. He scored the winning point."

"It was a team effort; you can't win a game all by yourself."

"Too bad you'll graduate this year; they would have made

you team captain for sure," Lexi says while holding up the trophy for us to see.

"Oh gosh, we're all done with high school in a bit, another milestone to look forward to," Jai says, tousling Paquito's hair.

"Have you guys got any plans after graduation?"

"I'm taking Jai to Mexico this summer to visit my abuelita's ranch. What about you?"

"We're taking a gap year to travel and work abroad."

"That's great, Lexi; I'm so happy for you guys."

"Maybe we can check in with each other once in a while?" I casually throw in.

"Of course, Kobe. How about six months from now, same time, same place?"

"Same people," Lexi adds.

With that, we say our goodbyes and continue living our awesome queer lives.

Three Months Later

Roy Wilson

Summer holidays have started. It's scorching hot, and everyone is lounging on the beach, at the pool, or in the park. I'm not, though. I'm working my butt off, clearing tables and stacking dishes in a dishwasher. I'm a busboy, also known as a waiters' assistant. It means doing all the boring and dirty work without getting any of the tips people leave, or having the occasional flirt with a pretty customer. It's not a surprising finale to my already crappy year so far. Another thing to add to my list of grievances, or the sh*t list, as I like to call it. And it all started so well.

Me, Jake and Kobe, best mates since childhood, were strutting around the school like we owned it. And truthfully, we did. We were popular, revered and feared. The perfect ingredients for a successful senior year. Until Kobe started acting so weird. Ever since he got that detention on Saturday, and missed an important match, he didn't seem like himself. And worst of all, he started siding with that rank little bender Paquito, and his buddies from the GSA. Just weeks before, he spray-painted all those rainbow flags, which was his idea, by the way. The hypocrite.

But we got him good. We followed him to that storage closet, tied him up and gagged him. We almost got away with it if it weren't for that annoying snoop, Fairview, who caught us on camera. Our parents were called to school, and we had to apologise to Kobe and his boyfriend. 'Cause that's what Pussyto is these days: his boyfriend. To make matters worse we got suspended for a week. In my case, it meant spending day in and day out with my alcoholic stepdad, who's too lazy to lift so much as a finger to help around the house. There's a reason I'm always over at Jake's or Kobe's. Until Kobe turned on us, and now it's just Jake and me. Or, actually, it's just me. Jake's gone on holiday for three weeks, getting a tan on some Spanish beach while chatting up the senioritas. A holiday isn't on the cards for me. My mum works three jobs to make ends meet, and to fund her boyfriend's drinking problem. I'm saving up so I can get as far away from here as possible once I have enough money. I feel bad about leaving my mum behind, but she'll never leave that smelly booze hound of hers. I don't know how much longer I can take his attitude before I strangle him in his sleep.

I'm on my break now, finally catching my breath after running around all morning. Think I might take a walk in the park. There's a duck pond I can wade in. Just to cool down for a bit. I take off my shoes and socks and walk in. Luckily, I'm allowed to wear shorts at work, so I go a little further.

I'm knee-deep in water now, and it feels great. As I turn around, a family of swans swims by. Mum is followed by three fluffy grey chicks, and Dad is closing the ranks. As I wade through the water, Mum is startled by my presence. Before I can take one more step, she lunges at me. I know swans are incredibly strong and defensive when they feel threatened, so I dive, trying to get away. When I resurface, the swan family has moved on. Thank goodness I'm safe. But how on earth am I going to explain this at work? I can't show up soaking wet. As I ponder my latest predicament, I see something sparkle in the water. Could be a reflection of sunlight, but it looks like a huge, precious stone. I pick up a rock. It's translucent and emits a soft glow. Just as I'm about to put it down, I see someone. It's a guy in what looks like a yoga outfit. I'm probably suffering from a heat stroke, 'cause this doesn't make any sense. As I drop the rock, Papa Swan decides he doesn't trust me after all. He comes for me, honking and madly flapping his wings. I dive again, but this time I do not resurface. I hit my head on that rock.

Collin Haines

Here I am again. Same sh*t, different summer. Lisa and I broke up. No one saw it coming, including me. We were so close and so much in love. We spent nearly all of our free time together, which was such a change after dating Marty. Don't get me wrong, he's a great guy, but he's got so many interests. I just felt like one of his hobbies. He was especially obsessed with handball. Seeing him play always made me proud, though. He's a beast out there on the court, not letting anyone or anything get in his way. He's the fastest, most agile guy I've ever seen in a wheelchair. And top scorer on his team for the second year in a row. Wish I didn't have to compete with all of his other passions in life. I guess in the end, I got annoyed with playing second fiddle all the time. On the other hand, he thought I was too clingy. Last summer, we decided we were better off as friends. I was absolutely wrecked for weeks until Lexi introduced me to Lisa. She had just moved into the neighbourhood.

Lisa was a breath of fresh air compared to Marty. She's quite introverted, a great listener and emphatic to those around her. She encouraged me to take up some hobbies of my own, so that's how I got into yoga. Her mum is a dietician, so we adopted a healthy lifestyle based on the latest trends and insights in nutrition. Soon, we became inseparable; I truly thought I had found my soulmate until after graduation. She told me she's taking a gap year in an Ashram abroad, meditating and doing yoga. This is right up my alley, so I said I would gladly join her. But she would have none of it. She needed space to reflect on her life, and how could she do that properly, if she was dragging her past along with her. I suggested a long-distance relationship, but she argued it would be better if we both made a fresh start. So here I am, wandering around town like a lost soul with no purpose. This time, Lexi isn't around to take my mind off things. She and Kobe left for their first backpacking adventure. I'm happy for them. Their relationship has had its ups and downs over the past few months, but they came out stronger than ever.

Mum gave me some money to redecorate my room. A coat of fresh paint and some new furniture might actually lift my spirits a bit. A bedroom makeover is just what I need to let those countless memories of Lisa and me fade into the background. I went to a hardware store this morning and bought paint in three different earth tones. Since I've spent half of what Mum gave me, I need to get my hands on some used furniture. There is a lovely thrift shop in the centre of town, but it doesn't open until three. It's just past noon, so I have three more hours to kill. As I walk past the school, I notice a dumpster on the side of the road. Didn't they just renovate some bathrooms? I peer inside, but most of its contents are damaged, beyond repair, or not what I'm looking for. Then I see a mirror on top of a smashed sink. It seems to be in a fairly decent state. I think it will complement my vintage vanity table perfectly. I lean over the side and grab the mirror with both hands. That's weird, it's glowing. I lean in a bit closer and take a good look. Staring back at me is a guy in shorts, standing in the middle of a duck pond. Have I gone insane? As I inch closer to having-a better look, I lose my balance. I tumble in headfirst, hoping with all my heart I won't crack my new mirror.

The End